Benjamin Barrett

The New View of Hell

Benjamin Barrett

The New View of Hell

ISBN/EAN: 9783337390327

Printed in Europe, USA, Canada, Australia, Japan

Cover: Foto ©Andreas Hilbeck / pixelio.de

More available books at **www.hansebooks.com**

THE

New View of Hell.

SHOWING

ITS NATURE, WHEREABOUTS, DURATION, AND
HOW TO ESCAPE IT.

BY

B. F. BARRETT,

AUTHOR OF "LECTURES ON THE NEW DISPENSATION," "THE GOLDEN REED,"
"LETTERS TO BEECHER ON THE DIVINE TRINITY," ETC., ETC.

PHILADELPHIA
J. B. LIPPINCOTT & CO.
1872.

LIPPINCOTT'S PRESS,
PHILADELPHIA.

CONTENTS.

PREFACE.

THERE are few subjects within the compass of revealed or speculative Theology, upon which inquiring minds have been more exercised within the last hundred years, than the subject of Hell. And there are few, perhaps, which have been the occasion of more strifes and divisions in the churches, which have caused more trouble to Christian believers, or upon which there are at this moment more anxiety, doubt and disagreement among religious teachers themselves.

There is no doubt that the popular mind of Christendom has undergone a considerable change on this, as on many other subjects, since the commencement of the present century. The old representations of the Divine justice, and of the condition of the wicked in the great Hereafter, would hardly be listened to with patience—certainly not with satisfaction—by any intelligent Christian congregation of to-day.

"The idea which men once had of hell and of divine justice," says the distinguished occupant of Plymouth Pulpit, "was a nightmare as hideous as was ever begotten by the hellish brood itself. And it was an atrocious slander on God. I do not wonder that men have reacted from these horrors—I honor them for it."

But what have the Christian teachers of to-day to offer as a substitute for the old idea, which is confessedly becoming obsolete in nearly all of the churches? Many of them, nothing—literally *nothing*, that can at once satisfy the reason of thoughtful inquirers, and meet the demands of the language of Scripture. And some are frank enough to confess their destitution. Said a distinguished Presbyterian clergyman, writing on this subject some time ago: "It is all dark, dark, dark, to my soul; and I cannot disguise it."

The aim of the present work is to unfold and present the New view of Hell, as set forth in the theological writings of EMANUEL SWEDENBORG; to show that it is at once rational and Scriptural, in harmony with the perfect love and wisdom of God, as well as with the teachings of human experience and the profoundest spiritual philosophy; and that its practical influence upon the character of believers, cannot be otherwise than beneficent.

How far I have succeeded in this, the reader himself must judge. But if I have achieved even a partial success, and presented the subject in a light to relieve and profit only a few troubled souls, I shall be more than satisfied—I shall be thankful.

B. F. B.

PHILADELPHIA, November 15, 1871.

NEW VIEW OF HELL.

I.

THE NEW DISPENSATION.

THE theological writings of Emanuel Swedenborg are regarded by many—by all, indeed, who have read and studied them with care—as a new revelation. They boldly claim for themselves this distinction, and challenge a candid examination of their claim in the light of Scripture, reason, philosophy, history, and all human experience. They are held to be (and this, too, is their own claim) a new Dispensation of spiritual truth: that Dispensation referred to in the Apocalypse under the symbol of the New Jerusalem which John saw coming down from God out of heaven. They are believed to contain, not merely the reasonings and conclusions of a great and pious mind—not a theological or doctrinal system wrought out by patient labor and hard study, but a system of spiritual truth so luminous in its nature and so grand in its proportions, as to be itself the fulfillment of the prophecy concerning the second coming of Him

who is "the Light of the world." They are declared to
be a revelation of new and heavenly truth made by the
Lord himself through his own chosen servant, whom He
raised up and prepared for this work, and in due time
graciously and wonderfully illumined by his Spirit.

The stupendous system of truth, therefore, contained
in the writings of this man, is not to be considered his,
but the Lord's. He was but the chosen instrument to
receive and make known to men, truths which no amount
of labor or study could ever have enabled him to dis-
cover. Hear what the seer himself says on this subject:

"Since the Lord cannot manifest Himself in Person,
and nevertheless has foretold that He would come and
establish a New Church which is the New Jerusalem, it
follows that He will do so by means of a man who
can not only receive these doctrines in his understanding
but can also publish them by the press.

"That the Lord manifested Himself before me his
servant, and sent me to this office, that He afterward
opened the eyes of my spirit and so intromitted me into
the spiritual world, granted me to see the heavens and
the hells, also to converse with angels and spirits, and
this continuously now for several years, I affirm in truth;
as also, that, from the first day of that calling I have not
received anything whatever pertaining to the doctrines
of that Church from any angel, but from the Lord alone
while I read the Word." (*True Christian Religion*, 779.)

And elsewhere in his writings he repeats the same

statement—in substance if not in words. Thus in his
preface to the *Apocalypse Revealed*, he says:

"Any one may see that the Apocalypse could no how
be explained but by the Lord alone, since every word
of it contains arcana which never could be known without some special illumination and consequent revelation.
Wherefore it has pleased the Lord to open the sight of
my spirit and to teach me. It must not, therefore, be
supposed that I have given any explication of my own,
nor that even of any angel, but only what I have had
communicated to me from the Lord alone."

And in his treatise on "The Intercourse between the
Soul and the Body," he relates a conversation that he
once had with "a man of reason," explaining to him
how it was that from a philosopher he became a theolo-
gian. After telling him that it was "for the same reason
that fishermen became the disciples and apostles of the
Lord," adding that he also "from early youth had been
a spiritual fisherman;" and after explaining what this
means, and confirming what he says by citing passages
from the Word which speak of *fishermen*, unfolding at
the same time their spiritual meaning, his interrogator
"raised his voice and said:

"'Now I can understand why the Lord called and
chose fishermen to be his disciples; and therefore I do
not wonder that He has also called and chosen you,
since, as you have observed, you were from early youth
a fisherman in a spiritual sense, that is, an investigator

of natural truths. The reason that you are now become an investigator of spiritual truths, is, that these are founded on the former.' To this he added, being a man of reason, that 'the Lord alone knows who is the proper person to apprehend and teach or communicate the truths which should be revealed for his New Church.' "—Ibid. 20.

Swedenborg further claims that this new revelation made through him as a chosen medium, is in fulfillment of the prediction made by the Lord himself, concerning his second coming, which was to be in the clouds of heaven. This coming, he says, is not to be external and natural, cognizable by the eye of sense; but internal and spiritual, cognizable by the understanding and the heart. It is to be a coming of the Word of God, that is, of the deeper meanings of the Word—a coming of its spiritual or heavenly sense to the minds and hearts of men, and exerting upon them a new and renovating power. And the *clouds* in or upon which it is said He would come, are the clouds of Scripture—the obscurities, more or less dense, of the literal sense, in or upon which the spiritual and true sense comes as the sun's light through a cloud. To cite again his own language:

"It is the prevailing opinion at this day [1770] in every church, that the Lord, when He comes to the last judgment, will appear in the clouds of heaven with angels and the sound of trumpets; that He will gather together all who are then dwelling on the earth, as well as all who are deceased, and will separate the evil from the good, as a shepherd separates the goats from the sheep; that then He will cast the evil, or the goats, into hell, and raise up the good, or the sheep, into heaven; and further that He will, at the same time, create a new visible heaven and a new habitable earth, and on the latter He will cause a city to descend, which is to be called the New Jerusalem, and is to be built according to the description given in the Revelation (Ch. xxi.) of jasper and gold; and the foundation of its walls of every precious stone; and its height, breadth and length to be equal, each twelve thousand furlongs; and that all the elect are to be gathered together into this city, both those that are then alive, and those that have died since the beginning of the world; and that the latter will then return into their bodies, and enjoy everlasting bliss in that magnificent city, as in their heaven. This is the prevailing opinion of the present day, in all Christian churches, respecting the coming of the Lord and the last judgment."—*True Christian Religion*, n. 768.

And a little further on he says:

"*That the second coming of the Lord, is a coming, not in person, but in the Word which is from Him, and is Himself.*—It is written in many places that the Lord will come in the clouds of heaven; as Matt. xvii. 5; xxiv. 30; xxvi. 64; Mark xiv. 62; Luke ix. 34, 35; xxi. 27; Rev. i. 7; xiv. 14; Dan. vii. 13; but no one has heretofore known what is meant by the clouds of heaven,

and hence mankind have believed that the Lord will
appear to them in person.   But it has remained undis-
covered to this day, that the Word in its literal sense is
meant by the clouds of heaven ; and that the spiritual
sense of the Word is meant by the power and glory
in which also the Lord is to come. . . . Now since the
spiritual sense of the Word has been opened to me
by the Lord, and it has been granted me to be with
angels and spirits in their world as one of themselves,
it has been revealed to me that the clouds of heaven sig-
nify the Word in its natural sense ; and glory, the Word
in its spiritual sense ; and power, the effectual operation
of the Lord by the Word."—Ibid., n. 776.

There can be no doubt, then, about Swedenborg's
claim—extraordinary though it be, and incredible as it
may seem to those who have not examined his writings.
He claims to have been called of the Lord in an extraordinary manner, and to have been specially illumined
by his Spirit, to make a new revelation ;—a revelation,
that is, of new and heavenly truth concerning Himself,
his Word, the nature of heaven and hell, and the condition of different classes of men in the great Hereafter.
He declares that it is the Lord who opened the eyes of
his spirit ; that it is the Lord who taught him the true
meaning of the Word, and what doctrines to promul-
gate ; that the Lord had actually come (agreeably to his
promise), to establish a New Church by means of the
doctrines which it was given him to receive, understand

and publish to the world; that these doctrines were not his own—not the result of any labor or study on his part, nor received from any angel, but communicated to him by the Lord alone. "From the first day of that calling," he says, "I have not received anything whatever pertaining to the doctrines of the New Church from any angel, but from the Lord alone while I read the Word."

It is not my purpose here to enter upon any discussion of this claim, or to adduce evidence to show that it is well founded. The need there was of a new revelation at the time Swedenborg lived and wrote, as shown by the doctrinal beliefs and teachings in all the churches of his day; the luminous and extraordinary character of his theological writings; the sweet and heavenly and catholic spirit that they breathe throughout; the elevated and rational views they contain on all subjects—views that harmonize with the teachings of Scripture and reason and science, and with all we know of the laws of the human soul and the ways and workings of God's providence;— all these combine to force an acknowledgment of his claim from every intelligent and candid mind who thoroughly examines and understands his writings. Such an one admits his claim *because he cannot help it.* He finds the evidence so overwhelming, that it is easier to accept than to reject it. He sees that here is, indeed, a new revelation; that here is a system of spiritual truth so grand and harmonious and rational, so comprehensive

and majestic, and so admirably adapted to human wants
in this age, that it could have none other than God himself for its author. He accepts Swedenborg's teachings,
therefore, as a new Dispensation of spiritual truth, bear-
ing the impress of God's own finger. So abundant and
overmastering is the evidence, that he cannot do otherwise ; he cannot reach any other conclusion.

But those cannot admit his claim, who have not studied
his writings. How can they ?—for they have not weighed
the evidence ; they have not seen it, indeed. And nowhere but in his writings themselves, can satisfactory evidence of his claim be found. They may, from having read
a few pages or chapters of his works, admit that he saw
and taught much truth ; but we cannot expect them to go
beyond this—nor ought they—until they have studied
his writings sufficiently to enable them to discern, in some
measure, their wondrous depth and comprehensiveness
and philosophy and unity. Such persons, (and they are
not a few) stand toward this New Christian Dispensation
in the same attitude as those stand toward the first Christian dispensation, who admit that Jesus Christ was a wise
and excellent man, and that much truth is to be found in
the New Testament ; but who do not admit the proper
divinity of the one, nor the inspiration of the other ;
who regard the Saviour as a merely finite and human
being, and the writings of the Evangelists as merely
human compositions. And while some of these persons
may have more of the spirit of Christ than many who

know and believe more of Him and his gospel, still they would not be regarded, popularly or doctrinally speaking, as Christians; for they do not acknowledge Christianity as a new Dispensation, or in any proper sense as a new Revelation.

So, popularly speaking, those are not of the New Christian Dispensation (they may belong to it *really* but not *nominally*) who do not see or acknowledge that any such dispensation has commenced, or that the writings of Swedenborg are, indeed, a new and divinely authorized revelation of heavenly truth—though they may have in their hearts more of the spirit and life of the New Church than some who accept its doctrines.

But many persons—and these inhabiting the most enlightened portions of Christendom—are beginning to admit that Swedenborg's claim is well founded. They believe that he wrote under a special divine illumination, and that his writings are or contain a new revelation. And what is implied by this admission? That no mistake, however trivial, is anywhere to be found in his writings? That in every sentence and word he penned after his illumination, he was immediately directed by the Lord? That every word he wrote is as certainly true as if it had been written by the finger of God himself? Nothing of this sort is involved in the fullest and most cordial admission of his claim. We may admit his divine illumination; we may believe that he was enlightened and taught

2 *   B

of God as no other man ever was; and that his writings are,
as they claim to be, a new and divinely authorized revelation; and yet we may believe that his illumination
was not precisely the same at all times; that he was not
absolutely infallible; that his pen, and even his thought
on some minor points, might momentarily have slipped,
making him teach or seem to teach in one place, something contrary to his general teaching upon the same
subject.

But an admission of this man's claim, or the belief
that his writings are a new dispensation of spiritual truth
to men, *does* involve the belief, that, upon all important
doctrines—upon all questions which have hitherto engaged the attention of Christians, and in which they are
likely always to feel a deep interest—he has spoken with
authority, because he wrote under an extraordinary divine
illumination.   It involves the admission that, in what he
wrote and published concerning the Lord, the Sacred
Scripture, Redemption, Regeneration, Salvation, the
Resurrection, the Judgment, the nature and duration of
Heaven and Hell, and all the great facts and laws of the
spiritual world, he has not given us his opinion merely,
but the truth which God was pleased to reveal through
him.   It involves the belief that, upon such momentous
themes he was illumined by the Holy Spirit, and has
taught only what the Lord authorized and directed him
to teach.   So that what his writings contain on such
subjects, is not his own opinions or conclusions merely,

but is what *the Lord himself teaches* or is *trying* to teach mankind through him.

Let me endeavor to make my view more clear by an illustration :—

A man is duly accredited by our government to the court of St. James. Upon all important matters between the two countries, he receives his instruction from Washington. And if he acts according to his instruction, the things he does as the authorized agent of the government, are not to be regarded merely as *his* acts, but the acts of the government; and the government alone is responsible for them. But in carrying on some negotiation, Mr. Adams or Mr. Motley, in the exercise of the freedom and discretion of a plenipotentiary, may here and there drop a word or use an expression which his government might not approve ; but that is of small consequence if it does not prevent nor in any way interfere with the negotiation. He may not, in every interview with the British minister of foreign affairs, or at every court dinner, do and say exactly the thing that the government from which he is accredited would approve ; but if he carries out his instructions generally, does his duty faithfully, and so accomplishes the purpose of his mission, is he any the less the accredited American minister, or his acts any the less cheerfully endorsed by his government because of an occasional and unimportant remark made by him, which the authorities at Washington might not approve ?

So Swedenborg—though it might be shown that he has here and there said things, unimportant in themselves but not in agreement with the general tenor of his teaching —is to be regarded as none the less a divinely accredited teacher or a divinely authorized expounder of sacred mysteries, if his teaching upon all important and fundamental points be true, or such as meets the approval of heaven's own King.

But though it is, or claims to be, a New Dispensation, it is a dispensation of *rational* religious truth. It addresses us as rational beings, endowed with the capacity of discriminating between right and wrong—truth and falsehood. It declares that Rationality, or the ability to understand spiritual truth when presented, and to judge between it and error, is one of the noblest gifts of God. And it holds it to be every one's solemn duty to respect this gift, by faithfully exercising his own understanding upon whatever is offered him for religious truth. It teaches that no one ought to accept what his own understanding rejects, even though it should be proclaimed by a messenger from heaven, or have the unanimous vote of all Christendom in its support.

No one, therefore, is expected to receive for truth what Swedenborg has taught on any subject, unless the teaching approve itself to his rational intuitions; that is, unless he himself sees it to be true. Each one must use his own eyes, and not allow another to see for him. The great seer himself says :

"This tenet, that the understanding is to be kept in subjection to faith, is rejected in the New Church; and in its place, this is to be received as a maxim, that the truth of the church should be *seen* in order that it may be believed. . . . What is truth not seen, but a voice not understood?" And again he says: "The angels have wisdom in consequence of seeing truths. Wherefore when it is said to any angel that this or that is to be believed although it is not understood, the angel replies, Do you suppose me to be insane, or that you yourself are a god whom I am bound to believe?"

This Dispensation, moreover, is catholic, comprehensive, universal, in its spirit. It breathes throughout the sweetest charity. It inculcates the largest liberty of thought. It encourages the utmost freedom of religious inquiry. It asserts with new and increased emphasis the great Protestant principle—the right of private judgment in matters of faith, however that judgment may differ from the solemn decree of popes, prelates, councils, synods, assemblies or conventions. It upholds, therefore, and furnishes new and powerful weapons in defence of religious liberty. It is tolerant of all forms of error, innocently imbibed and conscientiously held, and shows the possibility of salvation under all of them. It condemns no individual, no sect, no people—not even Mahometans or Pagans—merely on account of their beliefs; but teaches that infinite Love is for ever brooding over all; and for ever seeking, through such forms of faith and modes of worship as are best suited to the wants of each, to lift them up into clearer light and a higher life—into fuller communion and sweeter fellowship with itself. It is full, therefore—this New Dispensation— of the all-embracing and all-reconciling spirit of the Lord.

The following extracts—and a volume of similar ones might be quoted from the writings of Swedenborg—will exhibit something of the large and catholic spirit of this New Dispensation :—

"Notwithstanding there are so many various and different doctrines [believed by Christians], still, if all who hold these doctrines did but acknowledge charity as the essential of the church, or what is the same, if they had respect to *life* as the end of doctrine, they would together form one church; . . . for every one in the other life is gifted with a lot from the Lord according to the good of his life, not according to the truth of his doctrine separate from that good."—*Arcana Cœlestia* 3241.

"If charity were in the first place and faith in the second, the church would have another face. For then, none would be called Christians but they who lived the life of charity. Then, too, there would not be many churches distinguished by their different opinions concerning the truths of faith; but the church would be called one, containing all those who are in the good of life."—Ibid. 6761.

"Schisms and heresies would never have arisen if

charity had continued to live and rule in the church. For then they would not have called schism by the name of schism, nor heresy by the name of heresy; but they would have called them doctrinals agreeable to each one's particular opinion or way of thinking, which they would have left to his individual conscience; not judging or condemning any for their opinions, provided they did not deny fundamental principles—that is, the Lord, eternal life, and the Word—and maintained nothing contrary to the commandments of the decalogue."—Ibid. 1834.

"He who is in goodness of life does not condemn another because he differs from him in opinion, but leaves it to his faith and conscience; and he extends this rule even to those who are out of the church—[those, that is, in heathen lands]. For he says in his heart that ignorance cannot condemn any, if they live in innocence and mutual love."—Ibid. 4468.

"Within the church there are some of all denominations who have a conscience; though their conscience, however, is more perfect according as the truths which form it approach nearer the genuine truths of faith."—Ibid. 2053.

"Every one, of whatsoever religion he be, may be saved—even the Gentiles who have no truths from the Word—if only he has had regard to the good of life as an end."—Ibid. 10648.

"Let this truth be accepted and confirmed in the out-

set, that love to the Lord and charity toward the neighbor are the essentials of all doctrine and worship, then
heresies would be no more; and one church would be
formed out of many, however they might differ in doctrine and ritual. . . . In this case, all would be governed as one man by the Lord; for they would be like
the members and organs of one body, which, though
dissimilar in form and function, still have reference to
one heart, on which they all depend both in general
and in particular, however various their forms. Then,
too, every one would say of another, in whatsoever doctrine or external worship he might be, This is my brother; I see that he worships the Lord, and that he is a
good man."—-Ibid. 2385.

"Persons in a blind or persuasive faith, since they do
not see truths, are not willing that the doctrines of their
church should be approached and examined rationally
with the understanding; but they say that these are to
be received from a principle of obedience, which is called
the obedience of faith; and it is not known whether
the things received in such blind obedience be true or
false; nor can they open the way to heaven, for in heaven
nothing but what is seen, that is, *understood*, is acknowledged as truth."—*Apocalypse Explained* 1100.

"The dogma that the understanding is to be kept in
subjection to faith, is rejected in the New Church; and in
its place this is to be received as a maxim, that the truth
of the church should be *seen* in order that it may be be-

lieved ; and truth cannot be seen otherwise than *ration-ally.* How can any man be led by the Lord and con-joined to heaven, who shuts his understanding against such things as relate to salvation and eternal life? Is it not the understanding that is to be illumined and in-structed? And what is the understanding closed by religion but thick darkness, and such darkness, too, as rejects the light that would illumine ?''—*Apocalypse Re-vealed* 564.

These quotations might be extended indefinitely. But the reader may gather from the few here given, some-thing of the large, free, tolerant and truly catholic spirit of this new Dispensation. And if we recognize in nearly all the churches of to-day, a steady increase of this same spirit, that is only additional evidence that '' old things''—the old bigotry, narrowness, intolerance, denominational hatreds, and high partition walls of the last century—are passing away, and a new and more truly Christ-like spirit taking their place ; agreeably to the Divine promise : '' And he that sat upon the throne said, Behold I make all things new.''

3

II.

THE OLD DOCTRINE OF HELL.

MORE than a hundred years ago, Swedenborg announced the end or consummation of the first Christian Church or Dispensation, and the commencement of a new one. Repeatedly, and in the calmest and most emphatic language, did he declare that the Lord had manifested Himself to him in person; had opened his spiritual senses; had permitted him to see and converse with the denizens of the other world as men see and converse with each other; had vouchsafed to him a clear understanding of the spiritual and true meaning of the Sacred Scripture; and had authorized and directed him to make a new revelation of heavenly truth for the instruction of all Christians and for the benefit of mankind.

Up to this time comparatively few have openly embraced this new revelation. Yet its power has been seen and its influence felt in the gradual and steady modification of the old theological beliefs, which has been going on in nearly all of the sects for the last hundred years. This is admitted by some of the keenest observers and most advanced thinkers in all the churches. Says a learned critic of rare candor in the New York *Independent* (March 18, 1869):

" More than any other form of religious thought, Swedenborgianism is a leaven '*hid* in three measures of meal.' To a careless reader of ecclesiastical statistics, the Swedenborgian Church would seem to be one of the least of the great household of faith. To a careful student of religious thought, it appears to be among the most important. It has made very few converts from the faith of orthodoxy; but it has materially modified that faith. . . . As a little salt changes the contents of a large vessel of water, so Swedenborgianism, seemingly lost in the great multitude of churches, has more or less modified the form of faith of all."

And this very candid writer, and careful observer of the theological and religious tendencies of these new times, specifies some of the modifications already wrought in the old theological beliefs by the teachings of Swedenborg. After referring to the old doctrines of the Trinity, the Atonement, and the Sacred Scripture, and showing how these have been already modified by the writings of the Swedish seer, he concludes his list of specifications thus:

" The church [meaning all the so-called orthodox denominations] holds fast to the solemn truth, which no one has ever taught more vividly than Christ himself, that after death is the judgment, and after judgment heaven and hell; but it has accepted, unconsciously, from Swedenborg, his teaching that every man carries heaven or hell in his own bosom; and remits to the Past the fearful pictures of Edwards and his cotemporaries, of literal torments and a remorseless and pitiless God."

And with equal truth and plainness (though with a little less candor, perhaps, in not hinting at the real cause) the distinguished pastor of Plymouth Church (Brooklyn), said in a sermon on "Future Punishment" preached some months ago: "that the educated Christian mind of all lands, for the last hundred years [note the period] has been changing" in regard to the nature of punishment in the great Hereafter.

"It is certainly true," he continues, "that theories have been changing from gross material representations [of hell], more and more in the direction of moral representations. It is very true that this subject is not preached as it used to be—not as it was in my childhood. It has not been preached so often, nor with the same fiery and familiar boldness that it used to be. Multitudes of men who give every evidence of being spiritual, regenerate, devout, laborious and self-denying, find themselves straitened in their minds in respect to this question, and are turning anxiously every whither to see whence relief may come to them. There has been a profound change [within the last hundred years, observe] in the sentiment of Christendom in regard to those gross representations of future punishment, which were handed down to us from the past." And he gives, as among the reasons of those gross representations, "the mediæval literalization of the Bible figures."

Now, to judge correctly of the need there was of a new revelation a hundred years ago, we should go back to the time when Swedenborg wrote, and see what were the then accepted teachings upon the various points of Christian theology. Since that time the beliefs of Christians have, through the light of the New Dispensation (which is "as the lightning that cometh out of the east and shineth even unto the west"), become so modified, that, on many subjects, they bear but little resemblance to those held previous to that time. Very few are aware of the changes in theological opinion that have taken place in nearly all the churches during the last hundred years, and that are still going on at a rapid pace; and fewer still are aware of the cause of these changes.

Take, for illustration, the doctrine concerning hell, or the future punishment of the wicked. At the time Swedenborg wrote, the commonly received doctrine in all the churches was according to the literal teaching of the Bible. It was believed and taught for Christian verity that hell is literally a lake of fire and brimstone;—a *place* created by the Lord at the beginning for the express purpose of inflicting upon all who die in their sins as much suffering as infinite ingenuity could possibly devise. It was held that sinners, after death, were to be

3 *

cast alive into this burning lake by order of the Supreme Judge of the universe, as criminals on earth are cast into prison by order of the judges of criminal courts. And that they were always to remain there, perfectly conscious, indued with the most exquisite sensibility to pain, forever burning yet never consumed, writhing and groaning in eternal agony. And as if this were not torment enough, the gross imaginations of religious teachers often added other horrors equally revolting. Mr. Buckle, in his History of Civilization in England, speaking of the clergy of the seventeenth century—especially the Scotch clergy—and their view of hell and its torments, says:

" In the pictures which they drew, they reproduced and heightened the barbarous imagery of a barbarous age. They delighted in telling their hearers that they would be roasted in great fires and hung up by their tongues. They were to be lashed with scorpions, and see their companions writhing and howling around them. They were to be thrown into boiling oil and scalding lead. A river of brimstone broader than the earth was prepared for them ; in that they were to be immersed. . . . Such were the first stages of suffering, and they were only the first. For the torture, besides being unceasing, was to become gradually worse. So refined was the cruelty, that one hell was succeeded by another ; and, lest the sufferer should grow callous, he was, after a time, moved on, that he might undergo fresh agonies in fresh places, provision being made that the torment should not pall on the sense, but should be varied in its character as well as eternal in its duration.

"All this was the work of the God of the Scotch clergy. It was not only his work, it was his joy and his pride. For, according to them, hell was created before man came into the world; the Almighty, they did not scruple to say, having spent his previous leisure in preparing and completing this place of torture, so that, when the human race appeared, it might be ready for their reception. Ample, however, as the arrangements were, they were insufficient; and hell not being big enough to contain the countless victims incessantly poured into it, had, in these latter days, been enlarged. But in that vast expanse there was no void, for the whole of it reverberated with the shrieks and yells of undying agony. . . . Both children and fathers made hell echo with their piercing screams, writhing in convulsive agony at the torments which they suffered, and knowing that other torments more grievous still were reserved for them." (Vol. II. pp. 294, 295.)

Now every statement that Mr. Buckle here makes, finds ample confirmation in the works of distinguished theologians of that period and some of the previous centuries. Rutherford in his *Religious Letters*, speaking of the future punishment of the wicked, says: "Tongue, lungs and liver, bones and all, shall boil and fry in a torturing fire" (p. 17);—"a river of fire and brimstone broader than the earth." (p. 35.) And Boston, in his

Human Nature in its Fourfold State, treating of this same
subject, says: "They will be universal torments, every
part of the creature being tormented in that flame. When
one is cast into a fiery furnace, the fire makes its way into
the very bowels, and leaves no member untouched: what
part then can have ease when the damned swim in a lake
of fire burning with brimstone?" (p. 458.) And Rev.
Thomas Halyburton, in his *Great Concern of Salvation*,
says: "Consider, Who is the contriver of these torments.
There have been some very exquisite torments contrived
by the wit of men, the naming of which, if ye understood their nature, were enough to fill your hearts with
horror; but all these fall as far short of the torments ye
are to endure, as the wisdom of man falls short of that
of God." (p. 154, Edinburgh edit., 1722.)

Such was the generally accepted doctrine concerning
hell in all the Christian churches at the time Swedenborg wrote. Such, too, had been the doctrine for centuries previous, as we learn from Christian writers and
Christian artists. These latter aimed to embody or represent upon canvas the prevalent Christian thought of the
period in which they lived. Thus Michael Angelo, in
his picture of the *Last Judgment*, tells us more plainly
than words could tell, what idea Christians of his day
had of the future punishment of the wicked. Truly did
Mr. Beecher say in one of his sermons not long ago:

"If you will take this picture, you will better understand what was the real feeling of the age in which he

lived on the subject of reward and punishment, than by reading any amount of theological treatises. Let any one look at that; let any one see the enormous gigantic coils of fiends and men; let any one look at that defiant Christ that stands like a superb athlete at the front, hurling his enemies from him and calling his friends toward him as Hercules might have done; let any one look upon that hideous wriggling mass that goes plunging down through the air—serpents and men and beasts of every nauseous kind, mixed together; let him look at the lower parts of the picture, where with pitchforks men are by devils being cast into caldrons and into burning fires, where hateful fiends are gnawing the skulls of suffering sinners, and where there is hellish cannibalism going on—let a man look at that picture and the scenes which it depicts, and he sees what were the ideas which men once had of hell and of divine justice. It was a nightmare as hideous as was ever begotten by the hellish brood itself; and it was an atrocious slander on God. . . . I do not wonder that men have reacted from these horrors—I honor them for it." (*Plymouth Pulpit* for Oct. 29, 1870.)

And this bold and eloquent divine further adds in the same discourse:

"To allow such a stream of human existence to be fed and renewed in every generation, which was pouring over the precipice at the rate of thirty millions a year, into such torments as the old method of representation presented to us, and at the same time to teach that God was a loving Father—these two things have seemed so difficult to multitudes of persons, that they have fled from the attempt to reconcile them, and have abandoned all belief in them."

And how does Mr. Beecher himself reconcile them? Or how does he understand and interpret the language of the Bible which refers to the future state of the wicked? He frankly confesses his own blindness and confusion here. He don't know what to make of this language. "It goes to my heart to say these things," he says—i. e. the things he finds in the Bible. "Yet it is there, and if I am faithful to my whole duty I must preach it. As a surgeon does things that are most uncongenial to himself, so sometimes do I. And I do this with tears and with sorrow. It makes me sick."

It is plain, then, what was the old and universally received doctrine among Christians concerning hell at the time Swedenborg wrote.

Very few, however, believe this doctrine now. The light that has been flowing into all minds from out the new angelic heavens for the last hundred years, has so clearly revealed its hideousness, that you will hardly find an intelligent Christian of any denomination now-a-days, who does not reject it. Most people have no rational and clearly defined doctrine to take the place of the old; but this latter nobody now accepts.

The old doctrine, therefore, being such as we find it—

so irrational and monstrous and cruel in itself—so utterly repugnant to every true Christian feeling and to every just conception of the character and government of God —is it unreasonable to suppose that the Divine Being would some day vouchsafe a further revelation to his children on this subject? If there ever was a subject on which the minds of men were in utter and impenetrable darkness, and on which, therefore, a further revelation was needed, is it not the very subject we are considering? And at what time should we expect the revelation to be made, other than that when it seemed most necessary—the time of densest spiritual darkness, when such preposterous ideas as to the nature of hell and future punishment as those I have here presented, were generally taught and accepted for revealed truth?

III.

THE NEW VIEW.

WE have seen what the doctrine of hell was, which was generally taught and accepted by Christians a hundred years ago. It was a doctrine quite in agreement with the sensuous appearances of truth in the letter of the Word ; and in agreement, therefore, with the gross conceptions of men in a carnal and sensuous state. It taught that hell was, *literally*, a lake of fire and brimstone ;—a *place* into which the wicked were to be finally cast, not out of mercy to them, or from any consideration of their comfort, improvement, or best welfare, but from a feeling of Divine wrath and vindictiveness. It was the generally accepted belief when Swedenborg wrote, that this fiery lake was created for the express purpose of inflicting upon sinners the most excruciating tortures which Divine ingenuity could invent.

Moreover, according to the doctrine of that period, the Supreme Judge of all the earth took a fiendish delight in casting his rebellious offspring into that fiery gulf, listening to their agonizing shrieks, and gazing on their ceaseless and indescribable sufferings ! And no inconsiderable part of the joys of heaven, it was also believed and taught, would spring from a clear view, given to those there, of the dreadful torments of the damned, and from a contemplation of the contrast between the miserable condition of these latter, and their own happy condition in the realms of bliss !

Such was the dreadful doctrine taught from most if not all of the pulpits in Christendom a hundred years ago !—taught for the revealed truth of God !—taught by the professed expounders of the Word of God !—by the acknowledged teachers and guides of the people in matters pertaining to man's immortal life !

Yet intelligent people gravely ask, What need was there of any new or further revelation at the time Swedenborg lived and wrote ? Considering how the Word of God was then misunderstood and falsified by its professed expounders—in what fearful darkness the minds of professing Christians were then immersed, not only upon this subject but upon others also pertaining to religion, it would, indeed, have been strange if a new revelation *had not* then been made.

Nor need we wonder, in view of this horrible doctrine concerning hell, which was commonly taught a hundred years ago for Bible truth (to say nothing of other doctrines equally revolting), that so many in Christian lands should have lost all faith in the Bible as a Divine revelation; and that many others who retain their faith, should have come to deny the existence of any hell whatever in the other world. Among the last and sure results of

4

false teaching, are suspicions, doubts, denials, and finally
the total eclipse of all faith.

See how good men—ministers of the gospel even—who
have not accepted the rational and heart-cheering truths
of the New Dispensation, are troubled even in this our
day by what they suppose the Bible to teach in regard to
the future state of the wicked.   Says the late Rev. Dr.
Barnes, one of the most distinguished of the Presbyterian
ministers of our country :—

" That any should suffer for ever, lingering on in hope-
less despair, and rolling amidst infinite torments without
the possibility of alleviation and without end ; that since
God *can* save men and will save a part, He has not pro-
posed to save all—these are real, not imaginary, difficulties. . . . My whole soul pants for light and relief on
these questions.   But I get neither ; and in the distress
and anguish of my own spirit, I confess that I see no
light whatever.   I see not one ray to disclose to me why
sin came into the world ; why the earth is strewn with
the dying and the dead ; and why man must suffer to all
eternity.   I have never seen a particle of light thrown
on these subjects, that has given a moment's ease to my
tortured mind. . . . I confess, when I look on a world
of sinners and sufferers—upon death-beds and grave-
yards—upon the world of woe filled with hosts to suffer
for ever ; when I see my friends, my family, my people,
my fellow-citizens—when I look upon a whole race, all
involved in this sin and danger—and when I see the

great mass of them wholly unconcerned, and when I feel
that God only can save them, and yet He does not do so,
I am struck dumb. It is all dark, dark, dark, to my
soul, and I cannot disguise it."

How many other good men are there among the Christian ministers of to-day, who, if they would but confess
the honest truth, would tell you that they are in just the
same darkness and distress that Dr. Barnes here confesses
to—if not upon the same subjects, then upon some others
no better understood. Yet Dr. Barnes himself, I presume, was so confirmed in all the dogmas of the Presbyterian church, that the light of heaven as it beams out
from the luminous pages of Swedenborg, would have
seemed to him darkness as thick, perhaps, as that in
which he confessed himself to be;—it could hardly have
seemed *more* dense. Verily, "the light shineth in darkness, and the darkness comprehendeth it not."

Certainly, then, a new revelation concerning the nature
of hell, or concerning the condition of the wicked in
the great Hereafter, was greatly needed when Swedenborg wrote; and therefore it was to be expected.

Let us now examine the New doctrine on this subject,
and see whether it is really worthy of the origin claimed
for it; or whether it be as irrational as the Old one
which it comes professedly to displace.

. According to the new doctrine of the immortal life,
the human soul is in the same form as the material body
—that is, the human form. It is organized of spiritual

substance, as the natural body is of material substance. It is the real individual—man, woman or child. It is that in us which thinks, remembers, reasons, loves. It is endowed with the senses of seeing, hearing, feeling, etc. —far more acute and perfect, too, than the bodily senses. It is not subject to decay or death, but lives on after the natural body dies. When that change which we call death (and which *is* the death of the body) takes place, the soul passes consciously into the spiritual world. It was there before death, but *un*-consciously while its outlook was into the realm of nature; just as the body in a state of sleep is, unconsciously, in the natural world; and when it awakes, it becomes fully conscious of its abode here.

While the soul tabernacles in the flesh, its senses are ordinarily closed; but when released from all connection with the body, its senses are all opened. It awakes to a consciousness of its existence in the spiritual world. It is then brought into open and sensible intercourse with the people and objects of that world. Its eyes and ears being opened, it sees and hears other spirits as plainly as we see and hear one another.

And when the body dies, the character of every soul is, and continues to be, essentially the same as it was before death. And every one's character depends on the nature of his supreme or governing purpose—that is, on the character of his ruling love. If he were wise and righteous before death—if he took delight in serving and blessing others, he will be wise and righteous after, will find still greater delight in serving and blessing, and feel a more intense desire to serve and bless. But if he loved himself supremely—if his chief aim in life was to get gain for himself alone, to secure his own ease, comfort and advancement, and promote his own welfare, careless of the welfare and the rights of others, he will be in precisely the same state after death; he will be just as indifferent to the wants, the woes, the welfare and the rights of others as he was before. If he had no genuine love of the Lord and the neighbor before, he will have none after. If meanness, dishonesty, lust, tyranny, hatred, contempt of others in comparison with himself, and selfish greed of gain, were in his heart before, he will be full of these same unclean and hateful vermin after. As it is written: " He that is unjust, will be unjust still; and he that is filthy, will be filthy still; and he that is righteous, will be righteous still; and he that is holy, will be holy still."

Heaven is within the soul; so says the new doctrine. It is essentially *a state of life*, not a *place;*—a state of supreme love to the Lord and the neighbor. It consists in the reception and exercise of the Lord's own unselfish love, which for ever seeks not its own, but the welfare and happiness of others. The happiness of heaven results from the exercise of unselfish love. This love is the angels' breath of life; and the purer and more intense it is, the more exalted is their bliss.

4 *

We see how well this agrees with the teaching of our
Lord. For not only does He tell us that the sum of all
which the Law and the Prophets teach, is comprehended
in the two great commandments which require us to love
the Lord supremely and our neighbor as ourselves, but
He says also that "the kingdom of God is *within* you."
And the kingdom of God is the same as the kingdom of
heaven. Wherever love—pure, unselfish love—reigns,
there the Lord reigns; there his kingdom is established
and his laws obeyed.

And as the kingdom of heaven is within, so also (says
the New doctrine) is the kingdom of hell. As heaven
consists essentially in love to the Lord and the neighbor, which is the love of doing good and serving, so
hell consists essentially in the opposite kind of love—in
the love of one's own self; and this love is real hatred of
the neighbor.

Hell, therefore, is a state of life the very opposite to
that of heaven. It is a state in which the love of self
has absolute dominion in the heart. This love is the
fountain of all other evil loves. It is the primal source
of all infernal deeds. When it reigns supreme in the
heart, there is no evil thing which a man will not do
unless restrained by force, or by fear of loss, suffering or
damage of some sort. Hence the Lord says: "For out
of the heart proceed evil thoughts, murders, adulteries,
fornications, thefts, false witness, blasphemy"—all the

things which defile a man, or render him spiritually unclean.

We see, then, where hell is and what it is, according
to the New doctrine. It is in the soul, and consists essentially in the supreme love of self which prompts to all
infernal deeds. To have hell in the soul, or to be in a
state of supreme self-love, is to be *in hell;* just as having
heaven within, or loving the Lord supremely and the
neighbor as one's self, is to be *in heaven.*

Now all men are by natural inheritance more or less
selfish. Naturally, therefore, we are all in the low state
denoted by hell; for we are dominated more or less absolutely by the love of self. This is a low—a merely animal love; and as our corporeal or animal life unfolds
and matures, this love also unfolds and strengthens; so
that when we have attained to full maturity, it is usually
the strongest—the ruling love. But this is not our true
state. It is not the properly *human* state. It is not the
orderly or blissful state for which we were created. It
is not the state in which the Lord desires that we should
remain, because He desires that all should be happy.
Therefore He is in the constant effort to lift us out of
our carnal selfish state, and to make us unselfish and
loving like Himself. For this end He assumed our
natural humanity. For this end He has revealed the laws
of our higher or heavenly life. For this end He has
shown us very clearly the way to rise out of our natural
state of self-love, which is hell, into that higher and

nobler state—that state of sweet unselfish love, which is heaven.

This great change (for it is, indeed, a great change), or this passing out of a low, natural, selfish state of life, into one that is higher, richer, nobler—in short, into the truly human state, is spoken of in the Bible as a "resurrection to newness of life;" as a "putting off of the old man, which is corrupt according to the deceitful lusts," and a "putting on of the new man, which after God is created in righteousness and true holiness;" as "passing from death unto life;" as being "born again" —"born from above"—"born of God," without which, we are assured, no one can enter the kingdom of heaven. "Except a man be born again, he cannot see the kingdom of God."

Now although the Lord desires that we should all pass out of our low or hellish state, into that high and heavenly one which He has made us capable of attaining, although He has told us how we may do so—has made the way very plain—has assumed our nature with all its hereditary and selfish proclivities that He might thereby become to us THE WAY—yet He uses no compulsion. He leaves all in freedom to either remain in their low natural state, which is hell, or to rise out of it into that exalted and unselfish state, which is heaven. He has made known the conditions upon which alone we can rise; and He is ever ready to lend us all needed help. He is continually calling to us and saying, This is the way; walk ye in it. But He does not take hold of us like a policeman, and *force* us to walk in that way. No one *can* be forced to heaven; for no one can be forced *to shun evils as sins*, nor *to love what is good and true for its own sake.* To go to heaven, we must *freely* comply with the conditions; and the conditions are, that we voluntarily obey the laws of the heavenly life;—that we struggle with and overcome our selfish and evil propensities;—that we deny self, take up our cross, and follow the Lord in the regeneration.

Such, briefly, is the New doctrine concerning hell— where it is, what it is, and how to escape it. Is there anything in it absurd and revolting, as we have seen that there is in the Old? Is there anything here against which enlightened reason utters its emphatic protest?— anything which impugns the wisdom or love of our Heavenly Father?

But how does this doctrine, it will be asked, accord with the teaching of Scripture? It may be reasonable— far more reasonable than the Old doctrine. But is it also Scriptural? This is the question—and an important one it is, too—which next claims and will receive attention.

IV.

I HAVE said that while the Old doctrine of hell is sensuous, and in agreement with a sensuous philosophy and a sensuous interpretation of Scripture, the New is eminently spiritual, and in harmony with the higher spiritual philosophy and with the spiritual interpretation of the Word.

For the essential difference between the Old and the New doctrine, lies in this : That the Old represents hell as a *place*, created by the Lord at the time of man's creation, previous to his lapse into sin, and for the express purpose of tormenting sinners ; while the New declares it to be a certain internal *state*, wrought out in freedom through the voluntary infraction of the soul's own laws, or the laws of our higher life.   Your child may reside in the same *place* with yourself—beneath the shelter of the same roof, and surrounded by the same beautiful objects. But by a course of willful disobedience or unreasonable self-indulgence, that child may have destroyed its health, impaired its senses, and rendered itself miserable and wretched generally.   And until its habits are changed

46

and its health renewed, it will find rest and comfort in no *place* however beautiful.

Both hell and heaven, according to the New Theology, are *within* men. They are not *places* but *states of life*. But in the other world, these states project themselves outwardly, making all the surroundings of each spirit a perfect mirror, as it were, of himself;—reflecting with mathematical precision his own affections and thoughts. Heaven is a state the very opposite of hell; as opposite as day is to night, light to darkness, health to sickness, love to hate, good to evil. The essential life of heaven, is the life of disinterested love—love to the Lord and the neighbor. The essential life of hell, is the life of self-love; and this is real hatred of the neighbor. Heaven is a state in which the understanding is illumined by the light of truth; hell is a state in which it is obscured by the darkness of falsity. Heaven is a state of spiritual health, order, peace and joy unutterable; hell is a state of spiritual sickness, disorder, unrest and comparative sorrow. In the most exalted heavenly state, every one loves others even more than he loves himself; in hell, and in all hellish states, every one hates others in comparison with himself. Heaven is a state of humility, self-forgetfulness, and of sweet and serene trust in the Lord; hell is a state of pride, self-seeking, and inward alienation from and opposition to the Lord. Heaven is a state of the most delightful freedom, in which every one finds his highest gratification in the performance of good uses from love to the Lord and his neighbor; hell is a state of spiritual thraldom, in which no useful act is performed from love of or delight in the use, but only by compulsion, as a slave works under the lash.

It should be said, however, that the love of self is evil and makes man an infernal only when it is the supreme and ruling love. Then it is out of its place and the soul is in disorder._ In its right place, which is a state of subordination and complete subjection to the nobler love of heaven, it is good and useful. Says Swedenborg:

" These three loves [the love of heaven, the love of the world, and the love of self] are related to each other like the three regions of the body, the highest of which is the head, the intermediate the chest and abdomen, while the legs and feet and soles of the feet form the third. When the love of heaven forms the head, the love of the world the chest and abdomen, and the love of self the feet with the soles of the feet, then man is in a perfect state according to creation, because the two lower loves then subserve the highest as the body and all its parts subserve the head." (*True Christian Religion*, 403.)

But when the love of self or of the world is as the head—is supreme—then the true order is reversed; the man is turned, as it were, upside down; the love of heaven is as the feet, and he tramples on the laws of justice and neighborly love as often as his ruler (self-love) dictates.

Such, according to Swedenborg is the essential nature of heaven and hell. They are both within the human soul, and consist in essentially opposite states of life—opposite kinds of love—resulting by inevitable sequence, in character, conduct, modes of government, and an outward or objective world, as different as are the loves that rule in these two kingdoms respectively.

Surely there is nothing unreasonable in all this. But how does it agree with the teachings of Scripture? That is the question for present consideration. And the first thing that claims attention, is the meaning of the word *Hell*. To ascertain this, we must go to the original languages of the Bible.

SHEŌL AND HADES.

The Hebrew word translated *Hell*, is *Sheōl*. And Sheōl, according to its primary literal import, means *the under world*, or *a vast subterranean place pervaded by thick darkness*. Hence this word is sometimes translated *the grave*, as in Genesis xxxvii. 35 ; xlii. 38. The corresponding Greek word is *Hades*. This has the same meaning as Sheōl, and is always used instead of it in the Greek version of the Old Testament. And as further evidence of their identity of import, we find the passage from the sixteenth Psalm, "Thou wilt not leave my soul in hell" etc., quoted in the Acts of the apostles (ch. ii.).

5   D

And in the Old Testament the Hebrew word for *Hell* in this passage is *Sheōl*, and in the New it is *Hades*,—proving that these words have one and the same meaning.

Such being the plain literal import of the Hebrew *Sheōl*, and its Greek equivalent *Hades*, some theologians have contended that our English word *hell* ought to be restricted in its meaning to the natural world; for, according to the strictly literal import both of the Greek and Hebrew word, it means simply *the grave*, or *a low and dark place*—a place *underground;* and has no reference whatever to the condition of the wicked in the other world, or to anything beyond the natural realm.

And if the Bible is to be literally interpreted—if it contains no meaning beyond that which lies upon the surface, and which is obvious to the merely natural or sensuous mind, these theologians certainly have the best of the argument. What answer can the literalist consistently give? For how, according to his theory, is this word *hell* made to refer to the condition of the wicked in the other world? Why should it not be restricted in its meaning, to that which it literally denotes, viz., the *grave*, or *a dark subterranean region ?*

Yet there are insuperable difficulties which those who contend for such a limitation of the meaning of this word, have to encounter. For, to be consistent in their hermeneutics, they should limit the meaning of the term *heaven* in precisely the same way. They should insist on restricting the meaning of this word also to the realm of nature; and should maintain that it has no reference to the condition of the righteous in the other world—for, in its obvious literal sense it has not.

The word in the original Hebrew, translated *heaven* in our English version, is *shâmayim;* and the literal signification of this is, *the firmament*, or *the space above the earth*. It comes (so the best linguists tell us) from an obsolete root, *shâmâ*, whose meaning in the cognate Arabic language is, to be *high*, or *lifted up*. And to this Arabic radical lexicographers refer the Hebrew term as denoting an elevated locality—a *high place*. The Greek equivalent of this Hebrew word is *ouranos*, which is also translated by our English *heaven*, and means the same as *shâmayim;* that is, the space above the earth, or the vast concave that surrounds the earth. And according to most philologists it comes from the Greek radical *orao*, which means to *see*—referring to the space above or around the earth, where by means of the sun's light objects are visible.

We find, therefore, that the words *heaven* and *hell*, which occur so often in the sacred Volume, refer—in their plain, obvious, *literal* sense, as gathered from the Hebrew and Greek terms—to merely natural localities; one, to a place that is *high*, or to a region *above* the earth, involving also the idea or possibility of clear-seeing; the other, to a place that is *low*, or to a region *beneath* the earth, involving also the idea of darkness, or great difficulty in seeing. And if the literalists, or those who deny that the Scripture everywhere contains a spiritual sense, would be consistent, they should restrict the meaning of both these words to the natural world—and to things *without*, not *within* the soul of man. For all good Biblical scholars know that neither *heaven* nor *hell*, according to the literal import of their equivalent Greek and Hebrew terms, conveys an idea of anything above the realm of nature.

But there is abundant Scripture evidence that these terms are *not* to be thus restricted in their meaning. There is evidence that they refer to states and conditions of two widely different classes of people in the spiritual world. Thus the seer of Patmos tells us of persons and things that he saw *in heaven*, when he was "in the spirit," or when "a door was opened" to him in heaven. Surely the myriads of angels whom he beheld, were not seen with his natural eyes, nor in that region of natural space above our earth. No: John's spiritual eyes were opened, and this enabled him to see the beings and objects of the spiritual world.

The Apostle Paul tells us that, on a certain occasion, he was "caught up to the third heaven," and heard there things which natural language cannot express. How "caught up"? Was the apostle's material body lifted through natural space into the upper regions of the air? No one, I presume, believes this. No one supposes that his corporeal part underwent any change of place. No doubt there was to the apostle the appearance of being suddenly lifted up; but this appearance was caused by, and was in perfect correspondence with, a change which took place at that time in the condition of the apostle's own mind. It was produced by a sudden opening of his spiritual senses even to the third degree.* No one ever was or ever can be carried to heaven—the heaven of which the Bible speaks—by being elevated bodily to the upper regions of space;—no, not even if he were lifted higher than the stars.

Then in the parable of Dives and Lazarus, we find the rich man represented as alive and *in hell* after the death and burial of his material body; which proves conclusively that the hell of which the Bible speaks, is not any region of natural space, but the state or condition of the wicked—and a state, too, in which they find themselves *after* the death of the body.

How, then, are we to arrive at the true Scripture im-

---

* According to Swedenborg, man is endowed with spiritual senses, which are ordinarily closed during his sojourn in the flesh. Yet these senses may be and sometimes are opened during his abode on earth; and when opened, he is intromitted into the spiritual world, and sees the objects and hears the sounds of that world as plainly as with his natural senses he sees and hears the objects and sounds of the natural world. And if the spiritual senses are opened to the third or inmost degree (for there are three degrees to the mind corresponding to the three angelic heavens) the individual is thereby intromitted into the third or highest heaven. This, Swedenborg tells us, is the way in which he was admitted into heaven while on earth. And it was the way in which Paul was "caught up."

5 *

port of the terms *heaven* and *hell?*—for in their obvious
literal sense, they are both used to designate natural
localities—one a *high* and *illumined*, the other a *low* and
dark place. According to what principle or law is their
true meaning to be elicited?

Swedenborg answers this question, as no one else has
ever answered it. (Let the reader, if he would appre-
ciate the full force of the answer, bear in mind that the
Bible everywhere represents heaven and hell as opposite
kingdoms—opposite as light and darkness, love and hate,
truth and falsity, righteousness and sin, happiness and
misery)—He tells us that the written Word is composed
throughout upon the principle of correspondence; that,
between all natural and spiritual things, there is a correspondence like that existing between the body and the
soul; and that the Sacred Scripture, therefore, in each
and all its parts, contains both a spiritual and a natural
sense, which stand related like the spiritual and the natural worlds, or like the soul and body of man. The
spiritual sense is as the soul; the natural sense, as the
body. As the body's life is from the indwelling soul or
spirit, so the life of every part of the written Word is
from the spiritual sense. The body of man without the
soul, has no life; neither is there life in the letter of the
Word when divorced from its inner spiritual meaning.
It is by virtue of their spiritual sense that the Lord's
words are spirit and life; for he says: "The words that
I speak unto you, they are spirit and they are life." And

the apostle also clearly recognizes the same truth when he says: " The letter killeth; but the spirit giveth life."

Agreeably to this doctrine of the Sacred Scripture, therefore, the words *heaven* and *hell* have each a natural sense such as I have already explained, and a spiritual sense with which the natural corresponds. Natural space corresponds to spiritual or mental state. Hence all words of Scripture, which in their natural sense refer to space, in their spiritual sense denote states of the mind. Accordingly there is natural elevation, and spiritual elevation; elevation in space and elevation in state. And the term *heaven*, which in its natural sense refers to elevation in space, in its spiritual sense denotes elevation of state; —that exalted condition of mind and heart, that state of clear perception of whatever is beautiful and true, and of disinterested love for all that is good and right, in which the angels are.

So, too, there is natural lowness, and spiritual lowness; the former having reference to space, the latter to state. And the term *hell*, which in its natural sense denotes a low place or a region under ground, in its spiritual sense denotes a low groveling state of mind;—that state of carnal desire and selfish craving and obscure perception and blunted moral sensibility, in which the devils are.

We often use the words *high* and *low* in their spiritual sense in familiar discourse; and always when we have occasion to apply them to moral or human qualities, though in their primary literal signification they have reference only to natural space. We employ them to designate superiority and inferiority of character, or of mental and moral attributes. Thus we speak familiarly of a *high* order of intellect, of a *high*-minded man, of *lofty* souls, *superior* worth, *exalted* wisdom and love. We say of an individual that he stands *high* in the community, *high* in the church or in the state, that he is *above* others, etc., when our meaning is that he is spiritually or mentally above them—superior in wisdom, skill, integrity, and moral worth. And equally often in familiar discourse is the word *low* used in a similar way. As when it is said of a mean and selfish man, that he is a person of a *low* mind, *low* desires, *low* motives, or that he is a *low* fellow. Indeed, the correspondence between the natural and spiritual import of these terms, is so obvious that it has never been lost sight of. Every one perceives it from common influx.

The Lord is called the *Most High* in Scripture, and is said to dwell *on high, above* the earth, and *above* the heavens. Surely it is not with any reference to natural locality that such things are predicated of the omnipresent One. No rational mind thinks of interpreting such language literally; for no one thinks of localizing the Divine Being. He is in all space—in the depths beneath as truly as in the heights above—yet is Himself without space. But on account of the infinite purity and excellence of his character—because, in respect to the human attributes of love, wisdom and power, He is infinitely exalted above men and angels, He is said to be above all the earth, above the heavens, the Most High, etc.

Yes :—The Scripture has everywhere a deeper meaning than that of the letter. It was given, not to teach us natural but spiritual truth. And it is by means of the law or rule of correspondence now revealed, that its true spiritual meaning is to be elicited. Space corresponds to state. And the words *high* and *low*, therefore, which in their natural sense refer to opposite regions of space, in their spiritual sense denote opposite mental states— opposite kinds of love. The Lord is spiritually the Most High. Therefore those who draw near to Him spiritually, who become like Him in the spirit and temper of their minds, are spiritually exalted. And because all the angels are images and likenesses of Himself—because they resemble Him in their love, wisdom and works— because their affections, thoughts, motives, purposes are all pure, noble and elevated, therefore they are said to dwell *on high;* or, what is equivalent, *in heaven.*

And on the other hand those who are spiritually most remote from the Lord, who are most unlike Him in disposition and character, whose aims are altogether selfish, whose affections, thoughts, motives and actions are low and ignoble, and contrary to the nature of the Divine Love, and who are, therefore, in a state the very opposite to that of the angels, are said to dwell in a *low place, beneath the earth;* or what is the same, *in hell.*

I have said, moreover, that the Greek word translated

heaven, involves the idea of light, being derived from a verb which signifies *to see;* and that the original word translated *hell,* involves the idea of darkness, being composed of two words, which together mean *impossible to see,* or where one cannot see. Here, again, let that magic Key, the law of Correspondence, be applied; and observe the result.

Light and darkness, like all other objects, have a twofold signification—an outer and an inner, or a natural and a spiritual meaning. Light in its natural sense, is the light of the natural world, which affects our natural organs of vision. But spiritual light is of a different nature, though in perfect correspondence with the natural. It is the light of the spiritual world; and although in its essence it is divine truth, it appears before the eyes of the angels as light. They see by means of it. This light proceeds from the Lord who is the Sun of the spiritual world—a Sun that appears to the angels immeasurably more brilliant than the sun of our world appears to us. It is the light of this spiritual Sun which illumines the minds of both angels and men. This is "the true light which lighteth every man that cometh into the world."

And as natural darkness is the absence of natural light, so spiritual darkness is the absence of spiritual light. But there are two causes of natural darkness; one is the absence of light, and the other is a diseased state of the organs of vision. The darkness from the first of these causes is seldom of long duration; and if the organs of vision are preserved in a healthy condition, we shall be able to see when the light comes. But the darkness produced by the second cause is, indeed, deplorable. However brightly the light may shine, it is (if the eye-sight be gone) as if the sun were blotted out. The brightness of noon-day is as midnight darkness to us.

So, likewise, there are two corresponding causes of spiritual darkness. One is, the absence of truth, or spiritual light. But this kind of darkness may soon be dispersed. For a person may be ignorant, and therefore in spiritual darkness; yet he may preserve his mind in such an honest and healthy condition, that he will be able to understand and receive the truth so soon as it is presented to him. But there is another and far more deplorable kind of spiritual darkness. It is that which results from disobedience to the known laws of the heavenly life. It is the darkness into which those fall, who, under the influence of selfish and evil loves, confirm themselves in various false ideas contrary to the revealed Word of the Lord. For everywhere and always is it true, that "he who doeth evil hateth the light, neither cometh to the light lest his deeds should be reproved." Persons who, under the prompting influence of infernal loves, disregard and trample on the laws of their inner life, and so obscure their moral perceptions, come at last to hate the light of truth, and shun it as owls and bats shun the light of day. Their understanding becomes

diseased; their mental eye, adjusted to error. And however bright the truth may shine, they do not see it. To
them it appears as falsity. They "put darkness for light
and light for darkness." Therefore the Lord says: "If
thine eye be single [or more correctly, *sound, healthy*]
thy whole body shall be full of light; but if thine eye be
evil [i. e., *un*-sound, *diseased*], thy whole body shall be
full of darkness. If, therefore, the light that is in thee
be darkness, how great is that darkness!" Matt. vi.
22, 23.

Agreeably to this, Swedenborg often tells us that the
denizens of heaven dwell in light inconceivably more
brilliant than the light of this world; while those in
hell live in great darkness—for their understandings are
darkened by innumerable falsities originating in evil
lusts. Milton had a perception of this great truth when
he sang:

> "He that hath light within his own clear breast,
>   May sit in the centre and enjoy bright day;
>   But he that hides a dark soul and foul thoughts,
>   Benighted walks under the mid-day sun,
>   Himself is his own dungeon."

There is a great darkness *within* all evil spirits, and this
produces the darkness *without;* for in the other world
everything without is but the reflection, under the great
law of correspondence, of the state or quality of life
within. But evil spirits do not appear to themselves to

be in such darkness as they really are. Neither do evil men, whose understandings are darkened by falsities originating in evil loves. They even imagine themselves in clearer light than others. And so do the devils think they see far better than the angels. But their light is the light of fatuity—the dim (yet mercifully accommodated) light of perverted natures—which, compared with the light that shines in heaven, is as the light from ignited coals compared with the splendor of the noon-day sun.

From what has been said, and from the correspondence of light and darkness, we may see why the Divine Saviour—the embodiment and living manifestation of the Truth—calls himself "the light of the world"; and why He says to those who had not previously known the truth, but had nevertheless kept themselves in a state to receive it, "They that sit in darkness and in the shadow of death, upon them hath the light shined." We may see also why it is said that "God is light, and in Him is no darkness at all"; and of the wicked, that "they walk in darkness," and will finally be "cast into the *outer* darkness where there is weeping and gnashing of teeth."

All who do not, while here on earth, resist and overcome their evil loves, find themselves in that "outer darkness" when they enter the other world; for through the indulgence of their evil lusts they shut out the light of God and the things of his wisdom from their minds. They are, therefore, excluded from the kingdom of

heaven, having no heaven, and no love for the things
which constitute heaven, in their hearts.   Whatever
truths they have ever known, they now reject and turn
away from, because such truths condemn their evil loves.
And so they immerse themselves altogether in falsities,
for these are in agreement with their evils.   Hence
there are endless strifes and bickerings among them ; for
each one fights for his own falsity, and calls it truth.
And the jarring discord and angry disputes among those
who are in falsities, joined also with mutual hatred,
derision and contempt, are what the *gnashing of teeth*
corresponds to, and what it, therefore, spiritually denotes.

GEHENNA AND THE LAKE OF FIRE.

But the Bible speaks of a *fire* in the great Hereafter—·
of the fire of hell, the everlasting fire, a furnace of fire,
a lake burning with fire and brimstone, etc.   And in
this hell-fire, or lake of fire, it is said that the wicked
will have their part.   And the rich man in the parable is
represented as saying, " I am tormented in this *flame ;* "—
and this, after he had died and was buried.

I presume few intelligent Christians now-a-days think
of interpreting such language according to the strict
sense of the letter—as it was interpreted a hundred years
ago.   They will tell you that this language is figurative,
though none of them may be able to tell precisely what
was meant to be conveyed by it.   But Swedenborg, in
his great doctrine of Correspondence, has furnished the

true key to its meaning. He has given us the spiritual
meaning of hell-fire, or the Gehenna of fire, and told us
what it is in the human soul that fire corresponds to.

But as the literal sense is the foundation of the spiritual, it is necessary always to give careful attention to
this first.

In the original Greek, *Gehenna* is the word translated
hell, where the fire of hell, or the hell of fire, is spoken of.
And *Gehenna* is a Hebrew word transplanted into the
Greek, with but little variation in its form.   It is composed
of two other Hebrew words, *Gai* or *Gē*, which means a
valley, and *Hinnom*, the name of a man.   The literal
meaning, therefore, of *Gehenna* is, *the valley of Hinnom.*
This valley was south-east of, and near to, Jerusalem.
The brook Kedron ran through it.   Here the Jews at
one time practiced the most impious idolatry.   They
had an image dedicated to Moloch, to which they offered
in sacrifice not only bulls, lambs, rams, etc., but even
their own children, who were placed in the arms of the
image previously heated by a fire within, and thus were
quickly destroyed.   On this account the place subsequently came to be regarded with such abhorrence, that
it was made the common receptacle of all the filth and
rubbish of the city.   The dead bodies of animals as
well as of the most notorious criminals, were there
thrown into one common heap.   And a fire was kept
continually burning to prevent the atmosphere from becoming pestilential—the worms, meanwhile, reveling in

a luxurious repast upon the remains of the rubbish which the fire failed to consume.

Here we have the primary, literal signification of the *Gehenna of fire*, which our translators have rendered *hell-fire*. It means the fire that burned in that loathsome valley of Hinnom. And as the last punishment and disgrace of condemned criminals was, to cast their dead bodies into that valley or that fire, the place came to be used as an appropriate symbol of the condition of those in the other world, who had violated, and persisted in violating, the laws of eternal love and justice revealed in the Divine Word.

But what is the precise spiritual meaning of this *hell-fire*, or *Gehenna of fire*, as elicited by Swedenborg's grand Key—the rule of Correspondence? And we must never forget that the spiritual meaning of Scripture, if we can ascertain what that really is, is its true meaning. For the Lord has himself declared that *his* words "are spirit and life."

What, then, is the spiritual correspondent of fire? Swedenborg answers, "Love." Love, he says, is spiritual fire or heat. Love is life; and every man, therefore, has some kind of love, because he has life. To wholly deprive him of love, would be to extinguish the vital spark—yes, to annihilate him. Love is the motive power in whatever a man thinks, wills, says or does. As heat is the proximate cause of all activity, germination, expansion and growth in the natural world, so love is the cause of all activity, germination, expansion and growth in the moral or spiritual realm. Deprived of all love, a man would be like the earth deprived of all heat —unproductive and dead. While the more passionately he loves any object or being—it may be a woman, it may be wealth, it may be literary or scientific fame, it may be civil or military glory—the more alive and active he is. See how the lower kinds of love—the purely selfish and worldly—the love of gold or glory, incite men to days of toil and nights of watchfulness! And the higher and nobler kinds—loves purer and more angelic—are the springs of action in all men's higher and nobler achievements, in all deeds done to improve and bless mankind. Take away all love from human hearts, and what would men do then? And the less passionately one loves, the more sluggish he is in thought and action—the less is he *alive*. So obvious is it that love is the quickener and enlivener of the human soul, the very fire of every man's life. And the character of each one, therefore, or the quality of his life, is according to the nature of this fire.

The correspondence between natural and spiritual fire, or natural and spiritual heat, is placed beyond a doubt when we reflect upon the fact that the body grows warm in proportion as any kind of love is enkindled or intensified in the soul. The love may be impure and devilish, such as those feel who are full of anger or revenge; still it produces bodily heat; the face reddens and the

circulation is quickened. Again, the body grows cold
as love departs, or as its activity ceases. All of which
proves that there exists, between natural heat or fire and
spiritual heat or love, a relation like that between cause
and effect. And this kind of relation is what Swedenborg means by Correspondence.

It is for the same reason, also, that the bodies of children and young persons are usually warmer than those
of the aged. They have more love in their hearts, or
their love is more active ; and this quickens the circulation of their blood. For a similar reason, again, we call
persons whose hearts are full of love and sympathy,
warm-hearted ; and those who seem to have no love for
anybody, *cold*-hearted. Then how often do we hear
Christians pray that the Lord would kindle in their hearts
a heavenly fire ! And sometimes they pray that He
would *warm* them with his love. For the same reason
we hear it said of an angry man, especially if his anger
breaks forth in deeds of violence, that he is *inflamed*,
burns with anger, is *all on fire*, etc. And does not the
internal fire at such times manifest itself in the countenance as well as in the gestures and tones of the voice ?

Furthermore, the wise man says : " A hot mind is a
burning fire." And the inspired Psalmist calls the Lord
" a consuming fire" ; and says that " a fire goeth before
Him, and burneth up his enemies round about Him."
Does any one believe that the Lord is *literally* a consuming fire ? or that He *literally* burns up his enemies ?

No: This language, like all of the inspired Word, is the language of correspondence. It contains a spiritual meaning. And in this, which is its true meaning, it expresses the intensity of the Divine Love, and its effect upon the wicked. Those who are in states of opposition to the Lord, change his love in themselves into its opposite; just as the deadly night-shade changes the sweet dews and sunshine into poison. They cannot receive his love as it is, because of their own state. They feel it as something wrathful, fiery, burning. *To them* it is as a consuming fire; for they change its nature at the moment of receiving it. In its origin all love is pure and good; for it is all from Him who is Love itself. But its quality or nature is changed in the recipient subjects. (*See Swedenborg's Heaven and Hell*, n. 569.)

Now there are in general two very different and even opposite kinds of love. There is a love of the Lord and the neighbor, which is good; and there is a love of self and the world, which, when it reigns supreme in the heart, is evil, and prompts to all kinds of wickedness. And one or the other of these loves bears rule in every man, spirit, or angel, and constitutes the very fire of his life. Good men and angelic spirits live in the former, and wicked men and evil spirits live in the latter kind of love. There is, therefore, a heavenly and a hellish love; or, speaking in the language of correspondence, there is a heavenly fire and a hell fire—the term *fire* denoting the love or delight which constitutes the life.

"Infernal fire," says Swedenborg, "is the love of self and the world; therefore it is every lust which springs from these loves; for lust is love in its continuity, since a man continually lusts after what he loves; and it is likewise delight, for what a man loves or lusts after, he perceives as delightful when he obtains it; nor is heart-felt delight communicated to him from any other source.

"Infernal fire, therefore, is the lust and delight which spring from the love of self and the world as from their fountain. The evils originating in these two loves, are contempt of others, enmity and hostility against those who do not favor them, envy, hatred and revenge, and as a consequence of these, savageness and cruelty. And in regard to the Divine, they consist in the denial, and hence in the contempt, mocking, and reviling of the holy things belonging to the church; and after death, when man becomes a spirit, these evils are turned into anger and hatred against those holy things. . . . These are the things signified by *fire* in the Word, where the wicked and the hells are treated of."—*Heaven and Hell*, n. 570.

The supreme love of self, therefore, according to the New Theology, together with all the unholy passions and malignant feelings which proceed from it, and the infernal delight felt in the indulgence of filthy lusts, is what is meant by *hell-fire* in the true spiritual sense. This is what the *Gehenna of fire* corresponds to; for the delight arising from the gratification of mean, base, and purely

selfish desires, is a flame supported by that heap of spiritual filth and rubbish, which renders the heart of man
unclean.

From what has now been said, the meaning of that
"lake of fire burning with brimstone" spoken of in the
Revelation, in which "the fearful, and unbelieving, and
abominable, and murderers, and whoremongers, and sorcerers, and idolaters, and all liars" shall have their part,
is sufficiently obvious. Brimstone corresponds to the
filthy lusts of the natural man. These, through un-
bridled indulgence, feed and support the flame of infernal love, as brimstone feeds and supports the flame of
natural fire. Such lusts are spiritual brimstone.

Those, therefore, who are immersed in evil concupis-
cences originating in the love of self, are in precisely
the state which corresponds to being in a "lake that burneth with fire and brimstone." Such a lake is a perfect
symbol, framed under the law of correspondence, of the
spiritual condition of the wicked. Hence it is said that,
in the great Hereafter, they will have their part in this
lake. They are in it now and here, but not so entirely
as they will be then and there.

But a *smoke* is said to issue from that lake. "The
smoke of their torment ascendeth up for ever and ever."
What does this mean?

If the *fire* and the *brimstone* are not to be literally interpreted, neither is the *smoke*. If the former are sym-

bols of something spiritual, the latter should be so likewise. And so, indeed, it is.

We know it is the tendency of all infernal passions
and propensities originating in the love of self, to darken
the understanding in spiritual things;—to obscure our
perceptions of what is just and true and good. While
the more unselfish a man is, the more reverently he heeds
the still small voice within him, the more earnestly he
strives to *do* the will of the Heavenly Father, the clearer
becomes his moral vision, the keener his perception of
the true and right upon questions involving the higher
and more permanent interests of humanity. Hence we
read: "If thine eye be single, thy whole body shall be
full of light; but if thine eye be evil, thy whole body
shall be full of darkness." "If any man will *do* his
will, he shall know of the doctrine whether it be from
God." "He that *doeth* truth, cometh to the light."
Which texts conspire to prove that purity of purpose and
the faithful *doing* of the truth, are indispensable to clearness of mental vision upon subjects of profoundest interest. But where the love of self is supreme, and there
is no regard for God or duty, and no respect for the
great laws of love and justice, there the understanding
is darkened; there the moral perceptions are obscured,
and the true and right are not seen. As saith the inspired penman: "The sun and the air are darkened by
the smoke of the abyss."

From this we may see what is meant in the spiritual

sense by "the smoke of the pit," and the smoke that "ascendeth up for ever and ever." It is that darkened understanding, that mental obscurity which results from the fire of a supremely selfish love, which is the fire of hell. And in the other world where all outward appearances correspond to internal states, a cloud of smoke actually appears round about infernal societies when they are seen in heavenly light.

Thus we see that the doctrine announced by Swedenborg concerning the nature of hell, however it differs from the *literal* teaching of the Bible, is in perfect agreement with the teaching of its spiritual sense. No candid mind can deny that it is, indeed, the very doctrine of the Bible on this subject, and in harmony with the whole scope of its teaching as well as with all we know of the wisdom of God and the nature of man.

Then look at its obvious, practical tendency. By showing hell to be a *state* instead of a *place*, it teaches every one to look within himself, at his own heart; to examine carefully his dominant love, his ends and aims in life, his ruling principles of action. It teaches us, moreover, what that state is: and that those, and those only, go to hell, who carry in their bosoms the loves that rule in hell; and therefore that those only escape it, who resist and overcome these loves. It shows us that only those shun hell, who shun as sins against God the indulgence of the dispositions and loves of hell;—who shun, from religious principle, all wicked arts and devices, all base and dishonest actions, all falsehood, fraud, deceit, revenge and hate, all dispositions and actions that tend to separate us from God and heaven and bring us into fellowship with devils. It teaches further, that if we do not, here on earth, strive *to do* the Heavenly Father's will, and so vanquish within us the loves of hell, we shall carry those loves with us into the other world, where they will burst forth with quenchless rage.

Thus the practical tendency of this doctrine is good, and only good. It tends to make men less regardful of self, and more regardful of God and duty;—more honest and sincere in their conduct, more kind and generous in their feelings, more correct in their principles, more exalted in their aims, more pure in heart and life.

HELL — THE CHOSEN HOME OF ALL WHO GO THERE.

THAT the reasonableness and truth of the New doctrine of hell may be more apparent, and the sharp contrast between it and the Old be more clearly seen—as well as its consistency with the perfect wisdom and love of God, something more must be said about that essential element of our humanity—freedom.

We have seen that the Old doctrine is based upon the literal teaching of Scripture wholly divorced from its living spirit; and that it is in harmony with the sensuous conceptions and sensuous philosophy of a by-gone Age; while the New is eminently spiritual, in strict accord with the spirit of the Word, and with the highest spiritual conceptions of the most enlightened minds of this New Age. The Old makes hell a *place*, and the casting into it a purely arbitrary and willful act of Omnipotence; the New declares it to be a certain *state of life* which each individual forms or develops for himself through the voluntary abuse of his own freedom and rationality.

Every one, therefore, who goes to hell, goes there as

freely as the tippler goes to the gin-shop, or the profligate to the brothel.

Here is one born, we will suppose, and living in a miserable, barren, dreary region, where there is little to delight the eye or regale the senses. Yonder is a rich and fertile country, charming to look upon, abounding in fruits and flowers, singing birds and running brooks, splendid habitations and magnificent gardens, with everything therein that can charm or gratify the senses. But the way to that beautiful country is over a rough road —across deep ravines and miry places—and sometimes through turbulent waters and up steep and slippery acclivities. But there is no other road to that delightful region. Whoever would take up his abode there, must encounter all the difficulties of the way. He must climb the precipices, and wade the bogs, and wallow through the miry places, and ford the swiftly running streams.

And the dweller in the desert, we will suppose, knows all this. Now he may have his choice :—he may remain in the dreary region where he was born, or, if he is willing to endure the hardships of the journey, he may go to yonder region so rich and fair, and snuff its balmy breezes for the remainder of his life, and gaze upon its beautiful scenery, and inhale its sweet perfumes and taste its delicious fruits. The choice is offered him ; and he is free to choose. He may stay where he is, or go to the land of beauty and promise. But if he goes, he must endure all the fatigues and hardships of the journey.

He must accept the conditions, else he can never reach there. The proprietor of the country uses no compulsion. He simply says: There it lies; and this is the way to it; and there is no other. Go or stay, as you please. But remember, the going involves labor and hardship. If you are willing to endure these, that beautiful country, or as much of it as you desire, shall be yours forever.

Let this desert region represent man's natural state, and the beautiful country yonder, the state which he is made capable of attaining through spiritual labor and conflict with the foes of his own household, and the illustration is complete. By rising out of or migrating from that state of life denoted by hell, we come into the state denoted by heaven. It is not by any change of *place*, nor through any exercise of immediate Divine mercy that this is effected. It is a purely spiritual migration. It is a passing out of a low or exterior spiritual condition, into a higher or more interior one.

And though this change of state is as much a matter of the individual's own volition as an act of natural migration, or a change of natural locality, and cannot, indeed, take place without the exercise of his own free choice, yet it has its laws or conditions; and without the observance of these the change cannot be effected. And no one can be *forced* to comply with the conditions. He is left to his own free choice. He may remain in Egypt, and delve there under the lash of his old task-masters, and get what comfort he can from the flesh-pots; or he may (if he choose) leave that country, and go to the land of promise—"a land of brooks of water, of fountains and depths that spring out of valleys and hills; a land of wheat and barley and vines and fig-trees and pomegranates; a land of oil, olive and honey."

But *if* he choose the latter course, he voluntarily places himself under the Lord's government and guidance, and may expect at times the chastening hand of paternal love to keep him in the right way. "Thou shalt also consider in thine heart, that, as a man chasteneth his son, so the Lord thy God chasteneth thee." He must endure all the perils and hardships of the journey. He must go "through that terrible wilderness, wherein are fiery serpents and scorpions and drought—where there is no water."

But multitudes choose to remain and *do* remain in Egypt. They are not willing to accept the conditions on which alone they can rise out of their natural into a heavenly state of life. They are not willing to deny self, take up the cross, and follow the Lord in the regeneration. They are not willing to deny themselves the indulgence of their selfish and inordinately greedy propensities. They have no desire and make no effort to overcome these propensities, or to bring them into due subjection to higher and nobler loves. They prefer to follow the bent of their inclinations, and to do as their pride and love of self and greed of gain and lust of power prompt.

Multitudes of this class pass from the natural into the spiritual world every year. Some of them ultimate their supreme selfishness here, in words and deeds befitting devils;—in falsehood, fraud, theft, blasphemy, adultery, murder and other abominations. But some of them are, outwardly, quite respectable people. Some of them are members of churches—professedly very religious; and at times, when they have some selfish end to serve, they are (on the outside, at least) kind and benevolent. But inwardly, at heart, they are supremely selfish. It is this class (and they are to be found among Christians to-day, as certainly as they were among the Jews eighteen hundred years ago) whom our Lord addresses when He says: "For ye are like unto whited sepulchres, which indeed appear beautiful outward, but are within full of dead men's bones and of all uncleanness. Even so ye also, outwardly, appear righteous unto men, but within ye are full of hypocrisy and iniquity." Every one's real character depends on the quality of his heart—on the nature, that is, of his ruling love. All whose ruling love is the love of self, are devils at heart, though they may be saints to outward appearance.

Now the Lord does not desire to punish these people in any way—either in this world or in the world to come. He does not desire that they should suffer, nor permit them to suffer, except for their own ultimate good. He

forever desires to improve their condition, and perpetually works toward this end. But He cannot overcome
their inordinate self-love without their willing co-operation. Before He can do this, they must recognize this
love as essential evil when it is allowed the mastery, and
must compel themselves to deny its cravings and to obey
the laws of neighborly love. So far is the Lord from
hating these people, or from any desire that they should
suffer one atom beyond what He knows will be for their
own good, He pursues them with his infinitely wise and
pitying love, in the other world as He had previously
pursued them in this.

On their first entrance into the spiritual world, they
find themselves attended and cared for by wise and loving
angels. And the angels remain with them and perform
for them every kind office in their power, so long as
their company is agreeable, or so long as the new-comers
are willing that they should remain. But soon their interior selfishness becomes active. Their internals come
forth into their externals. Their devilish dispositions
and feelings manifest themselves in corresponding looks,
words and actions. Their interior and real character
throws off whatever mask it had previously worn on
earth, and reveals itself as it really is. The previously
hidden or concealed quality of their hearts comes out
there, and is openly and fully revealed. Agreeably to
these words of the Lord : " For there is nothing covered
that shall not be revealed, neither hid that shall not be

known." Their externals are brought into perfect agreement with their internals; and they show by their looks,
tones, words and actions, just what they are. They no
longer have a divided mind; but they appear outwardly
just what they are inwardly. The avenues in their souls
through which they had previously held some communication with heaven, or retained some perception of
heavenly things, are all closed—closed in tender mercy
to them.

Is it not infinitely better for a wolf, that he be wolf
all through, from inmosts to outmosts? Suppose the
wolf possessed a kind of human internal, which enabled
him to see the dreadful ferocity and cruelty of his nature, and filled him with keenest self-reproach every time
he invaded the sheep-fold. Suppose he were human inside, but wolf outside; yet the wolfish propensities were
so strong and overmastering that they could not be held
in check. Can we not see what unutterable misery that
poor creature would endure?

It is from tenderest mercy to the selfish and inwardly
evil, therefore, that, in the great Hereafter the heavens
of their minds are closed; that their moral sense, or
their perception of right and wrong, is completely benumbed or lost; and that their externals are reduced to
a state of perfect agreement with their internals. When
this takes place, they no longer desire to remain in company with the angels. The angelic sphere becomes extremely disagreeable to them—painfully so; and they

withdraw from it as instinctively as owls and bats withdraw from the light of day. And then they gravitate each one to the society of spirits whose character
is nearest like his own. For in the hells as in the
heavens there are innumerable societies, some in one
kind of evil and some in another; and some more desperately wicked than others—for there are various kinds
and degrees of wickedness in the other world, as there
are in this. And the great law of spiritual affinity, which
is as universal and constant in the spiritual world as the
law of gravitation is in this, tends to bring those of like
character together, and to hold them together.

Every evil spirit, therefore, soon as his interior character is fully developed, gravitates with unfailing certainty toward those who are most like himself. Nor
does he go reluctantly among his like; he goes there
willingly, gladly, joyfully, as thieves and profligates on
earth go among those of like character. He seeks their
society in perfect freedom, because he finds it congenial;
because he *prefers* it to the society of the good and wise;
and he prefers it, *because they are like himself.* With
them he feels more at home, more free, more contented,
more happy than any where else;—and it is the Lord's
ceaseless desire and effort to make every one as happy as
possible. He does not force a single individual to go
where he does not wish to go in the Hereafter. And
those who go into any of the societies of hell, go in freedom and from choice. They go there because they find

such society more congenial than that of the angels.   If *forced* to live in heaven, or in the society of the wise and good, they would be out of their proper element; nay, they would be unspeakably miserable.   It would be far more cruel than it would be to compel persons whose eyes are diseased, to dwell in the bright blaze of the noon-day sun.   Accordingly Swedenborg says:

"Spirits who come from the world into the other life, desire nothing more than to be admitted into heaven. Almost all seek to gain admittance, imagining that heaven consists only in being introduced and received.   Therefore also, because they desire it, they are conveyed to some society of the lowest heaven; but when they who are in the love of self and the world approach the threshold of that heaven, they begin to be so distressed and tormented interiorly, that they feel hell in themselves rather than heaven.   Therefore they cast themselves down headlong thence; nor do they find rest until they come into hell among their like.

"It has often happened also that such spirits desired to know what heavenly joy is; and when they heard that it is in the interiors of the angels, they have wished to have it communicated to themselves.   Therefore this also was granted,—for whatever a spirit desires, who is not yet in heaven or in hell, is granted him if it be beneficial.   But when the communication was made, they began to be tortured to such a degree that they knew not into what posture to screw their bodies on account of the

pain. I saw them force their heads down even to their
feet, cast themselves upon the ground, and there twist
themselves into folds, in the manner of a serpent; and
this by reason of the inward agony. Such was the effect
which heavenly delight produced upon those who were
in delights from the love of self and the world." (*Heaven
and Hell* n. 400.)

Again he says:

"Most of those who go from the Christian world into
the other life, carry with them the belief that they are to
be saved by immediate mercy. But when they are examined, they are found to believe that to come into heaven
is merely to be admitted; and that those who are admitted are in heavenly joy,—being totally unacquainted
with the nature of heaven and of heavenly joy. Wherefore they are told that heaven is not denied to any one
by the Lord; and that they can be admitted if they
wish, and tarry there as long as they please. They who
have desired this, have also been admitted; but when
they reached the first threshold, they were seized with
such anguish of heart, from the breathing upon them of
heavenly heat which is the love in which the angels are,
and from the influx of heavenly light which is divine
truth, that they experienced infernal torment instead of
heavenly joy; and in consequence of the shock they cast
themselves headlong thence. Thus were they instructed
by living experience, that heaven cannot be given to any
one from immediate mercy."—Ibid. 525.

We see this great law of affinity exemplified here on earth—among animals as well as the human race. Those of the same species or general characteristics, always prefer the society of each other. Beavers love to be with beavers, bears with bears, wolves with wolves, mice with mice. None of these creatures feel quite contented or at home in the society of animals of a totally different nature.

And so with the members of the human family. Not only do the evil, when left to act in perfect freedom, shun the society of the good, but they group themselves together according to the kinds and degrees of wickedness in which they are. Pirates choose the society of pirates; thieves the society of thieves; counterfeiters the society of counterfeiters; tipplers, gamblers, burglars, profligates, the society of persons of their own profession —persons most like themselves. So obvious is this truth, that it has passed into the proverbs, universally accepted, "Birds of a feather flock together;" and "A man is known by the company he keeps."

There can be no doubt, then, that this law of affinity is one of the unchangeable laws of the moral universe; and it must, therefore, govern in the arrangements of all in the spiritual world—the evil as well as the good. It must group congenial spirits into innumerable associations. And a most wise and beneficent provision it is, too;—a provision whereby every human being, whatever be his character, shall have a home in the Hereafter among just that class of persons whose society he prefers and finds congenial to his tastes.

But the societies of the hells, selfish and wicked as they are, are under a government as well as those of the heavens. And this government, too, is provided by the Lord, and is most wisely and mercifully adapted to their condition and wants. It is provided for the best good of the devils themselves, as well as for the good of all other parts of the moral universe. It is precisely such a government as they require; the only one, indeed, that is suited to their state—a government not of love, but of fear and force; for there is no love of the neighbor in their hearts, and therefore no desire to promote the common good. Hence their violent and malignant passions can only be restrained by fear of punishment. Says Swedenborg:

"All the inhabitants of hell are governed by fears; some by fears implanted in the world, which still retain their influence; but because these fears are not sufficient, and likewise lose their force by degrees, they are governed by fear of punishments, and this fear is the principal means of deterring them from doing evil. The punishments in hell are various, more gentle or more severe according to the nature of the evils to be restrained. For the most part, the more malignant who excel in cunning and artifice, and are able to keep the rest in a state of submission and slavery by punishments and the terror thereby inspired, are set over the others;

but these governors dare not go beyond the limits prescribed to them. It is to be observed that the fear of
punishment is the only means of restraining the violence
and fury of those in the hells. There is no other."
(*Heaven and Hell*, n. 543.)

Who cannot see that this is the very best kind of government for those in hell—the only kind, indeed, that is
suited to their state and needs? We see that punishment
there has a beneficent design and a beneficent tendency.
It is not directly from the Lord, though it results from
the unfailing operation of laws that He has established.

"Wherefore," says Swedenborg, "when evil is done
from an evil heart, then, because it casts away from itself
all protection from the Lord, infernal spirits rush upon
him who does the evil, and punish him. This may be
illustrated in some measure by crimes and their punishments in the world, where also they are linked together;
for the laws prescribe some punishment for every crime,
so that whoever rushes into crime, rushes also into the
punishment thereof. The only difference is, that in the
world crime may be concealed; but in the other life
concealment is impossible. From these considerations
it may be seen that the Lord does evil to no one; and
that the case herein is similar to what we find in the
world, where not the king, nor the judge, nor the law,
is the cause of punishment to the guilty, since neither of
them is the cause of the crime committed by the evil-
doer." (Ibid. n. 550.)

Look, now, at the intrinsic reasonableness of this New doctrine of hell; and compare, or rather contrast it with that believed and taught a hundred years ago. While our reason protests against the Old as utterly absurd, it freely and cordially accepts the New. The Old is a purely sensuous doctrine, in accordance with a sensuous age, a sensuous philosophy, and a sensuous interpretation of holy Scripture; while the New is eminently spiritual, in harmony with the conceptions of spiritually minded men, with the higher spiritual philosophy, and the spiritual interpretation of the Divine Word. The Old is arbitrary—lying quite outside of the domain of law and order; while the New is seen to be in perfect accord with the known laws of the human soul—the inevitable result, indeed, of the violation of these laws. The Old presents God as a very monster of cruelty; while the New exhibits Him as a wise and tender and loving Father, forever pursuing his rebellious children into the lowest depths of sin and suffering; clasping his arms around even the devils in hell; providing a congenial home for all in the great Hereafter; and *just such a home* as each one, by the life that he has voluntarily formed, strengthened and confirmed, is fitted to enjoy, and will himself *freely choose.*

Who, that is not utterly blinded by prejudice, can fail to see that this New doctrine, as compared with the Old and once generally accepted view, is as the light of noon-day compared with the darkness of midnight!

VI.

THE DURATION OF HELL.

HAVING shown where and what hell really is, and having exhibited the sharp contrast between the Old and the New doctrine in respect to reasonableness; —having shown, also, that the law according to which all spirits, the evil as well as the good, associate in the great Hereafter, is unquestionably a law of the human soul, and *must* therefore be as enduring in its operations as the soul itself, I proceed next to consider the momentous question :—

Is the condition of the wicked in the other world, as Swedenborg was permitted to see and commissioned to reveal it, to continue substantially the same throughout the ages of eternity? In other words, will those who pass into that world in a hellish state of life, remain for ever in that state? Or can men repent, and their ruling loves be changed from evil to good, after death? Can the great work of spiritual renewal be *commenced* in the other world (with those who have died in a state of confirmed evil), if it has not been begun in this? Or, as some believe and confidently affirm, are "the inverted forms of the natural degree which constitute the external

body of the infernal in the hells," to be finally destroyed
through "the unrestrained ultimation given to the ruling
infernal loves"?—so that the man (when these forms
are destroyed), "freed from his prison-house in the
hells," will be "restored to his original *infant* state of
conscious existence,"?—will "at once ascend to the plane
of the New Heaven—his eternal Home—and there, from
this new point of departure, advance in and to Eternal
Life"?

These interrogatories, it will be seen, are only different ways of presenting one and the same question, which
is commonly stated in this form: "Are the hells to be
unending in their duration?"—or this: "Will those
who go to hell after death, always remain there? Will
they always continue in an infernal state?"

This inquiry is not only natural, but it is one which
cannot be kept down. It rises spontaneously to the
thought, however its utterance by the lips or pen may be
suppressed.

And where shall we look for an answer to this question? To the intuitions of the natural reason? or to the
unequivocal teachings of Revelation? Is the verdict of
natural reason worthy of implicit reliance in questions of
this nature?—perverted, distorted, beclouded as all will
admit this reason to be. Were reason alone sufficient to
assure us of our continued and conscious existence after
the body dies? Reason may have nothing to urge
against the doctrine of the soul's immortality—nay, it

may have much to urge in favor of it; but could it *prove* it in such a manner as to give us anything like a comforting assurance of its truth?

And if unaided reason could not discern or clearly demonstrate even the soul's *existence* apart from the material body, what could it tell us about the nature, facts or laws of that realm which it is to inhabit after the body dies? What assurance could reason alone give us of any hell or heaven after the death of the body, or what could it tell us of the nature of either?—to say nothing of the more profound and subtle questions like that now before us. What need was there of any revelation concerning the life after death, if human reason of itself could have learned all about it?

Obviously the Lord saw the inadequacy of reason to such sublime discoveries; and therefore, in tender compassion and love toward us, He supplements the deficiencies of reason by the clearer light of revelation. He opens the eyes of chosen seers and prophets, and through them reveals truth concerning man's immortality and the life after death, which no one's reason without such revelation could ever have found out.

Plainly, then, the question before us narrows itself down to this: What is the teaching of revelation on the subject? Has the infinitely wise and gracious Lord— aiming to instruct and bless mankind through his own chosen and gifted seers—deigned to tell us anything in regard to the duration of the hells? If so, what is it?

Any one may reject the revelation, or refuse to believe it
if he chooses; but in that case he either denies that any
divinely authorized revelation has been made on the
subject, or he sets his reason above that revelation; he
assumes "to be wise above what is written," yea, wiser
than the Lord himself. He plants himself *outside* of or
above revelation, on precisely the ground occupied by
the Deistic and rationalistic schools. I cheerfully
concede every one's right to do this; but doing it, he
has no right to complain of the logical consequence.
He has no right to find fault with others for casting him
into the ranks of those whose fundamental idea he delib-
erately accepts.

Have we, then, a divinely authorized *revelation* on this
subject? And is that revelation clear and unmistak-
able? This is the question for those to consider who
believe in revelation; and my argument is addressed
exclusively to such. And it is a question which should
be approached with judicial calmness, and with as much
freedom as possible from the biasing or blinding influence
of our own private judgments, feelings, or wishes in the
case. The question is: Has the Lord spoken on this
subject? And if so, what has He said?

Nowhere but in its literal sense, does the Scripture tell
us anything about the duration of hell; for in the
higher or spiritual sense of the Word, no idea is anywhere conveyed of time or duration in the sense commonly understood by these words. And it cannot be

denied that, so far as the Bible in its literal sense teaches anything about the duration of hell, it teaches that it will be unending. The same terms to indicate endless duration, that are applied to heaven, are also applied to hell. Its punishment is said to be "everlasting," and its fire "the fire that *never* shall be quenched." "And these [the wicked] shall go away into everlasting punishment, but the righteous into everlasting life."

And the great majority of the First Christian Church have believed, according to the plain teaching of the letter, that the hell of which the Bible speaks is to be unending in duration, and that those who go there after death will remain there for ever. It is plain that the Lord intended that those who received his Word (as Christians have hitherto for the most part) in its literal sense, *should* believe in the eternity of hell. Otherwise, we may be sure that very different language would have been employed from what we find wherever the duration of hell is spoken of. And if it be argued, as it sometimes is, that the words "eternal" and "everlasting" are occasionally applied in Scripture to things known to be of temporary duration, and if the force of the argument be admitted, what follows? Why, simply that the Bible teaches nothing in regard to the duration of hell, and that no argument can be drawn from its language either for or against its eternity.

Let us turn, then, to that more recent revelation which

the Lord has been pleased to make for the establishment
and upbuilding of a New Christian Church;—a revelation wherein are disclosed many things concerning the
life after death, which the First Christian Church was
not able to bear.   Upon no one subject, perhaps, has the
Lord's servant been more explicit, than upon the duration of the hells.   The following are some of his clear
and emphatic statements :

"Every man's ruling affection or love remains with
him after death, nor is it extirpated to eternity; since
the spirit of man is altogether such as his love is; and
(what is an arcanum) the body of every spirit and angel
is the external form of his love, perfectly corresponding
to the internal form [i. e. to the quality of his love].
It is therefore manifest that man remains to eternity of
the same character as his ruling affection or love is.   It
has been granted me to converse with some who lived
seventeen hundred years ago, and whose lives are well
known from the writings of that period; and it was
found that every one was still influenced by the love
which ruled him when he lived in the world." (*Heaven
and Hell*, n. 363.)

"Man, as to his entire life [or character], remains for
ever such as he is at the time of his death." (Ap. Ex., n.
174.)   "As man is when he dies, such he remains to
eternity." (Ibid. 125.)

"It is man's will-faculty that lives after death, and not
his thinking-faculty except so far as this has been in

agreement with his will-faculty. . . . It may be imagined by those who are not instructed concerning the life after death, that they can then easily receive faith when they see that the Lord governs the universal heaven, and when they hear that heaven consists in loving Him and their neighbor. But they who are principled in evil, are as far from being able to receive faith after death, that is, from being able to believe from a ground in the will-faculty, as hell is from heaven. . . . If it were possible for spirits to believe and become good from mere instruction in the other life, there would not be a single individual in hell; for the Lord is desirous of elevating all, how many soever there be, to Himself in heaven. For his mercy is infinite, because it is the Divine [Love] itself; and is exercised toward the whole human race, alike toward the evil as toward the good." (*Arcana Cœlestia* 2401.)

"The life of a man cannot be changed after death, but must remain for ever such as it had been in this world; for the character of a man's spirit is in every respect the same as that of his love; and infernal love can never be changed into heavenly love, because they are in direct opposition to each other. This is what is meant by the words of Abraham addressed to the rich man in hell: 'Between us and you there is a great gulf fixed; so that they who would pass from hence to you, cannot; neither can they pass to us who would come from thence.' (Luke xvi. 26.) Hence it is evident that all who go to hell, remain there for ever." (*New Jeru-salem and its Heavenly Doctrine* n. 239:)

"He who is in evil in the world, is in evil after his departure from the world; therefore if evil is not removed in the world, it cannot be removed afterwards. Where the tree falls, there it lies. So also does a man's life, when he dies, remain such as it was. Moreover, every one is judged according to his deeds; not that these are recounted, but because he returns to them and does them as before; for death is a continuation of life, with the difference that the man cannot then be reformed." (*Divine Providence* n. 277.)

"Because it has been granted me during many years to be with the angels, and to speak with new-comers from the world, I can with certainty testify that every one is there explored as to the quality of the life he had led; and that the life which he contracted in the world remains with him for ever." (*Conjugial Love* 524.)

"Since it has been granted me for many years to be in company with the angels, and to converse with those who have left the world, I can testify with certainty that every one is there examined as to the quality of his past life, and that the life which he had contracted in the world remains with him to eternity. I have conversed with those who lived many ages ago, whose lives I was acquainted with from history; and I found them to be of a character similar to the description given of them.

I have also heard from the angels that no one's life can be changed after death." (*Brief Exposition* n. 110.)

"I have been told by the angels that the life of the ruling love [after death] is never changed with any one to eternity, since every one is his own love; wherefore to change that love in a spirit, would be to deprive him of his life, or to annihilate him." (*Heaven and Hell* n. 480.)

"I can testify from much experience, that it is impossible to implant the life of heaven in those who have led an opposite life in the world." Then—after relating some experiments made with persons who had imbibed the notion that they might receive the life of heaven in the other world, however they had failed to obey the laws of that life in this—the writer concludes: "From these and other experiments, the simple good were instructed that no one's life can possibly be changed after death; and that evil life can by no means be changed into good life, nor infernal life into angelic, since every spirit from head to foot is of the same quality as his love, and therefore of the same quality as his life; and that to transmute this life into the opposite, were to destroy the spirit altogether. The angels declare that it were easier to change a bat into a dove, or an owl into a bird of paradise, than an infernal spirit into an angel of heaven." (Ibid. n. 527.)

(See also *Arcana Cœlestia* n. 3762, 3993, 4464, 4588, 5145, 7186, 8206, 9061, 10,243, 10,284; *True Chris-*

tian Religion n. 531, *Doctrine of Life* n. 8, and other places, where the same doctrine is plainly taught.)

The above quotations and references (and many sim-ilar ones might be made), leave us in no doubt as to what the doctrine revealed for the New Church on this subject, is. I have quoted freely, that the reader may see how explicit and uniform and positive Swedenborg is in his teaching concerning the impossibility of any essential change of character taking place in the other world. The time in, which the several works here quoted were written, stretches over a period of more than twenty years; yet the essential fact stated is always the same. There is not a single point of doctrine on which he has been more explicit or more positive.

Nor does he proclaim the endless duration of the hells as his belief or opinion merely, but as a part of the reve-lation which he was divinely commissioned to make. And not only does he declare the fact over and, over again, and without any essential variation throughout the long period of his illumination, but he tells us that this is what the angels believe and teach on the subject, and is what is meant by the passage in the Word which speaks of a gulf that *cannot be passed over* after death. And not only so, but he assures us that he saw and con-versed with persons known to him from history, who had been dead, some of them seventeen hundred years, and some for ages, and whose characters had not essentially changed since that period. And elsewhere he tells us *why* the character cannot be changed after death, as will be shown in a future chapter.

Now no one is under obligation to accept Swedenborg's teaching on this or any other subject. He may accept or reject it as suits his inclination. But I submit that he cannot consistently accept this man as a teacher sent of God—as one divinely illumined and commissioned to make a new revelation—and at the same time discredit or reject such explicit teaching as we find in the foregoing extracts.

Can we suppose the Swedish seer to have been enlightened as no other man ever was upon spiritual subjects generally, yet more in the dark on this one—and by no means an unimportant one, either—than some of us who give no evidence of, and make no pretensions to, any special illumination? There is as little reason for believing him mistaken in regard to the duration of the hells, as there is for believing him mistaken in regard to a hundred other things that he tells us he was commissioned to reveal concerning the great Hereafter.

We cannot, therefore, reject Swedenborg's teaching on this subject, without virtually discrediting his claim as a divinely commissioned messenger, and claiming for ourselves a higher degree of illumination than he enjoyed—upon one subject, at least.

The eternity of the hells, then, is not a human invention. It is not the conclusion of natural reason, nor the offspring of an unenlightened mind. It is a matter of divine revelation, as much so as the immortality of the soul, the nature and time of the resurrection, the nature of heaven and hell, and the law that determines the associates of each one and the appearance of his surroundings in the Hereafter. Whoever rejects the doctrine, therefore, sets his own reason above revelation, or assumes to be "wise above what is written." Yet the revelation is not contrary to enlightened reason, but quite in accordance with it, as will be shown hereafter.

But let us suppose, for the sake of argument, that the hells are *not* to be eternal;—that, ultimately, all the devils will become, through a process that no one yet understands or is able to explain, shining and happy angels. Supposing this to be the fact, the time *may* come when the Lord will reveal it to the children of men. But certainly that time has not yet arrived. The Lord *has not yet* made such a revelation as justifies any man who plants himself upon revealed truth, in maintaining the non-eternity of the hells. What right, then, have we to preach, on such a subject, a doctrine which the Lord in his infinite wisdom has thought proper not to reveal— nay, a doctrine the very *opposite* to that which He *has* revealed? If it were best for the world in its present state that this doctrine be preached, certainly God would have known it, and would have vouchsafed the needed revelation. But since He has *not* done this, but *has* told us in the most explicit language that the hells are eternal —that a man's ruling love cannot be changed after death

—shall we assume to be wiser than the Most High, and proclaim in advance a doctrine, which (supposing it to be true) the Lord in his wisdom has thought proper hitherto to conceal from the children of men ?

No : Let us scrupulously guard against such presumption. Let us reverently acknowledge that the infinitely wise One knows what truth, or what measure of truth, is adapted to human wants, and what is the proper time to reveal it. Under the New Dispensation the Lord has plainly taught the eternity of the hells. True or not, it is clearly *His* will that it should be believed and preached —for the present, at least—yes, during the continuance of this Dispensation. And to believe or teach a different doctrine, is either to discredit the revelation that has been made, or to assume to know better than the Divine Being himself what is true on this subject, or when is the proper time to proclaim this truth.

We see not, therefore, how any one who professes to believe in Swedenborg's divine illumination—who regards him as a man especially prepared, authorized and sent of God to make a new revelation—can for a moment think of rejecting or questioning his teaching in regard to the duration of the hells, or of substituting for it the more than doubtful conclusions of his own understanding. Surely it is not wise to shut ourselves in a dark room and invoke the feeble glimmer of a lamp, when the great orb of day is shining in meridian splendor.

VII.

EVERY individual has some ruling love; and this
love is his life. His character is according to the
nature of this love;—heavenly if the love be good, infernal if the love be evil. And this love each one takes
with him into the other world, because he takes there his
life—his character—his own spiritual organism which
the ruling love has moulded; and he can take nothing
else.

And according to Swedenborg the ruling love cannot
be changed after death. If, therefore, it be of an infernal character, it remains so for ever. The individual will
have no desire to change his character in the other
world, or to be anything else than his ruling love
makes him; and without such desire we cannot conceive how any essential change in him can possibly take
place. And if the character or ruling love undergoes
no change after death, then the wicked will remain so
for ever, and the hells will be unending in their duration.

And this is the solemn fact disclosed by Swedenborg.

Upon no single subject is he more explicit in his teachings, than upon the unchangeable state of the wicked in
the other world, and the consequent eternity of the
hells. The extracts in the preceding chapter furnish
sufficient evidence of this. And although this question,
like all others concerning the life beyond the grave,
is one to be settled mainly by the light of revelation, yet
revelation rightly understood will ever be found in agreement with the highest reason. Let us, then, examine
Swedenborg's teaching on this subject in the light of reason and of that comprehensive system of spiritual philosophy which his own writings furnish.

Consider, first, what takes place with the evil in this
world ;—and by the evil I mean all those who act, not
from principle, or from any regard to what in itself is
just and right, but from purely selfish considerations.
We know that the love of self is strengthened by being
indulged ; and weakened only as its cravings are denied.
Like every other faculty and propensity, it acquires
strength by exercise. The more it is allowed to have
complete sway, and to outwork itself in all the multifa-
rious forms of villany—such as falsehood, fraud, theft,
adultery, murder—the more hardened does the soul become, the more benumbed its sensibilities, the dimmer
its perceptions and the feebler its desire for whatever is
true and just and right in itself. Let a person go on
cheating and defrauding from month to month and year
to year, and he will find himself steadily growing more

9 *

and more blind to the odiousness and moral deformity
of this vice, and less and less inclined to change his
course.   Or let him practice for a considerable time,
lying, stealing, profane swearing, adultery, or any other
vice, and his perception of its sinfulness will gradually
grow more and more obscure, and his inclination to turn
from it more and more feeble.

So with every sinful habit in which a man indulges.
The longer it is pursued the more fully does the evil inclination take possession of him, the more overmastering
becomes its sway, the darker his understanding, and the
weaker his inclination to return to the path of innocence
and rectitude. No fact is better established and no law
of the human soul is more certain than this.

Now, under the operation of this law, can we conceive
how spirits in the other world, when self-love, which is
essential evil, has taken full possession of them, so that
they are the very forms of that love ;—so that they turn
from and loathe the society of the good, and love and
seek the companionship of the wicked ;--so that they
put darkness for light and light for darkness, and say to
evil, "Be thou my good" ;—so that they hate and shun
the light of heaven as owls and bats shun the light of
day ;—so that they find their delight in doing evil, as a
wolf finds his in destroying sheep, or a hog his in wal-
lowing in the mire ;—so that they go *from choice* each
one to some congenial society in hell, as freely as the
tippler, the gambler and the profligate go to their chosen

haunts ;—when spirits, I say, are brought into this state, can we see in any rational light how they are ever to be brought out of it ? Can any one give us any rational or philosophical explanation of the *modus operandi ?* To suppose that they *may* be brought out some time or other and in some way or other, is scarcely less absurd than to suppose that a wolf may be changed into a lamb or a serpent into a dove. The supposition has neither reason, philosophy, experience, nor historical fact to support it.

If heaven could be given by an act of immediate mercy, undoubtedly all would finally go there ; and there would be no hell. But it cannot. It is an internal state which cannot be developed or reached without the individual's *own volition and active co-operation.* The heavenly character must be developed, the heavenly organism and tissues must be formed, else the light and warmth of that sweet realm would be as uncongenial as our atmosphere is to fishes, or as the light of the noon-day sun is to owls and bats. Agreeably to this Swedenborg says :—

" Many spirits entertain the opinion that heaven may be given to every one from immediate mercy ; and on account of their belief they have been taken up into heaven ; but when they came there, because their interior life was contrary to that of the angels, they grew blind as to their intellectual faculties till they became like idiots, and were tortured as to their will faculties so that they behaved like madmen ; in a word, they who go to heaven after living wicked lives, gasp there for breath, and writhe about like fishes taken from the water into the air, and like animals in the ether of an air-pump, after the air has been exhausted."—*Heaven and Hell*, 54.

Again he says:

"Conscience is the Lord's presence with man; and this is nearer in proportion as a man is in the affection of good and truth. If his presence is nearer than is suitable to the degree of a man's affection for good and truth, the man comes into temptation. The reason is, that the evils and falsities in him tempered with the goods and truths in him, cannot endure a nearer presence. This may appear from circumstances existing in another life, viz., that evil spirits cannot possibly approach any heavenly society without beginning to experience anguish and torment:—also that hell is removed from heaven, because it cannot endure heaven, that is, the Lord's presence which is in heaven. Hence it is said of them in the Word: 'Then shall they begin to say to the mountains, Fall on us; and to the hills, Cover us.' Luke xxiii. 30."—*Arcana Cœlestia* 4299. See also n. 4225, '6, 5057, '8, 4674, 7519.

It is in tenderest mercy to the wicked, therefore, that they are not compelled to live in heaven; for they would be far more wretched among the angels, than they are in their own chosen and congenial homes in hell.

But the heavenly life, some think, *will* be at last and gradually developed in the devils, so that they will all finally become angels. Again I ask, How? Will it be developed like vegetable life, without the volition or active co-operation of the spirits themselves? Is moral character ever developed or formed under the laws of the vegetable kingdom? *Can* it be? And are the conditions and surroundings and influences in the hells, and the kind of government that exists there, favorable to the development of the heavenly life? Or is this life to be gradually unfolded and strengthened there, *in spite* of all the adverse influences? If so, will any one tell us how. Will he show us the law, or give us some hint of the philosophy of this development.

But God, it is said, wills the salvation and happiness of all men. And can we suppose that His will is to be frustrated?—that He will not be able finally to accomplish his purpose?

And does not God will that men live righteously here on earth?—that they shun falsehood, theft, hatred, adultery, murder, as sins?—that they practice toward each other the laws of neighborly love? But is the Divine will accomplished? As a matter of fact, *do* all men live as the Lord wills that they should? And if not, then is not the Divine purpose so far frustrated? And if frustrated here and now, then why not there and always? No argument for the non-eternity of the hells can be based upon the omnipotence of the Divine will, unless it can be shown that this will with reference to man is *never* frustrated. And in order to show this, we must concede that all the abominable deeds which men commit, are done in accordance with the will of God. For if not, then the omnipotence of that will does not always ensure the accomplishment of the Divine purpose.

But the mistake arises from overlooking the proper characteristics of man, or the nature of the properly human faculties. If he were a machine, he might be dealt with as a machine; and the builder or operator would alone be responsible for its movements or defects. But being *man*, and endowed with the faculties of liberty and rationality, he becomes *himself* responsible for his actions and his character. His salvation and happiness are not things that can be *forced* upon him—no, not even by Omnipotence itself. They are states to be freely chosen, sought after, labored for, by himself; and in no other possible way can they ever be attained. If we could conceive of those, who have become so thoroughly confirmed in evil as to love and seek the companionship of devils, desiring and laboring for the exalted and unselfish life of heaven, then we might concede the possibility of the devils being all ultimately converted into angels, and the hells blotted out or changed into heavens.

Then there is a judgment which all have to undergo in the other world. And Swedenborg has described very fully the nature of that process. It consists in such a complete development of each one's internals, or such a thorough immersion of the individual in his own dominant love, whatever that may be, that he no longer has a divided mind;—no longer wears any disguise, or appears outwardly different from what he is inwardly. This judgment, or letting each man drop, as it were, into himself, takes place in the intermediate state, or world of spirits.   And it is accomplished by means of the all-revealing light of truth.   " The Word that I have spoken, the same shall judge him in the last day."   Swedenborg says :

" With the wicked, all those things which belong to the exterior thought from which they speak, and to the exterior will from which they act, are not properly theirs, but those things which belong to their interior thought and will.

" When the first state [after death] is passed through, which is the state of the exteriors, the spirit is let into the state of his interiors. . . . In this state he thinks from his own will, therefore from his own affection or from his own love ; and then his thought makes one with his will, and so completely one that he scarcely appears to think but merely to will.

" All men without exception are let into this state after death, because it is the proper state of their spirits. . . . When a spirit is in the state of his interiors, it manifestly appears of what character the man was in himself when in the world; for he then acts from his selfhood. He who was evil in the world, then acts foolishly and insanely—more insanely, indeed, than he did in the world, because he is in freedom and under no restraint.

"No one goes to hell until he is in his own evil and in the falsities of evil [or until there is a perfect union of will and understanding]; since it is not allowed any one there to have a divided mind, that is, to think and speak one thing and to will another. Every evil spirit must there think what is false derived from evil, and must speak from such falsity; in both cases from the will, thus from his own proper love and its delight and pleasure, as he did in the world when he thought in his spirit, that is, as he thought in himself when he thought from interior affection. The reason is, that the will is the man himself, and not the thought, except so far as it partakes of the will; and the will is the man's very nature or disposition; therefore to be let into his will is to be let into his nature or disposition, and also into his life, for man puts on a nature according to his life; and after death, he remains of such a nature as he had procured to himself by his life in the world, which, with the wicked, can no longer be amended and changed by means of thought, or the understanding of truth.

"Every one goes to his own society in which his spirit was while he lived in the world; for every man as to his spirit is conjoined to some society, either infernal or heavenly. . . . The spirit is led to that society by successive steps, and at last enters it. An evil spirit, when he is in the state of his interiors, is turned by degrees toward his own society, and at length directly to it before this [second] state is completed; and when completed, the evil spirit of his own free choice casts himself into the hell of those whose character is similar to his own."— *Heaven and Hell* 502–510.

We see from this that the judgment which every one undergoes after death, is merely the bringing of a man's externals into perfect agreement with his internals, or his thoughts, words and actions, into agreement with his ruling love. It is turning the "whited sepulchres" inside out. It is letting the man drop into himself; so that he no longer has a divided mind as he had when in the flesh, but is of the same character all through from centre to circumference. Unless, therefore, he is subsequently to undergo another stupendous change, of which revelation has told us nothing—unless he is to be brought back again into his former *double-minded* state, and the heavenly part of him then to be aroused into strong and persistent action so as to completely overpower the infernal part, we cannot see how he is ever to be brought out of his hellish state. For we must remember that there are no *germs* of heavenly life in man—no *"remains"* of good and truth implanted by the Lord—which can develop under the laws of vegetable growth, or without the individual's own volition. We know of no such involuntary development of the heavenly life in this world ; nor can we conceive of any such in the world to come.

Equally unphilosophical, too, and alike unsupported by reason and revelation, is the idea that, at some indefinite period after the judgment here referred to, the

10

sinner will die or be destroyed "that the *man* may be saved"—meaning by the *sinner* "the inverted forms of the natural degree, which constitute the external body of the infernal in the hells." There *is no such* "*sinner*" then and there, apart from the living, conscious, immortal individual;—no such "external body" that may be sloughed off, leaving "the man in his original infant state of conscious existence"—"the actual state of the infant man of the New Heaven." All this is mere theory, without the slightest foundation in fact, philosophy, or duly authenticated divine revelation.

Swedenborg's teaching, then, in regard to the eternity of the hells, is clearly in accordance with reason and the highest spiritual philosophy of which the world has any knowledge.

And the Bible, so far as it teaches anything on the subject, confirms the testimony of reason and philosophy. It speaks of the wicked in the Hereafter, going away "into everlasting punishment," while the righteous go into "everlasting life";—of a great gulf between the evil and the good, which cannot then be passed over;—of a fire that "never shall be quenched." It assures us that, in the other world, every one will be judged and rewarded according to his works. "The dead were judged out of those things which were written in the books, according to their works." "The word that I have spoken, the same shall judge him in the last day." The blessing of the higher, even the heavenly life, is promised to none but those who keep or do the Lord's commandments ; nor do we find in Scripture any warrant for the belief that others will *ever* enter in through the gates into the city ;—for what other way is there, save by religious obedience to the laws of the heavenly life ?

"Blessed are they that do his commandments, that they may have right to the tree of life, and may enter in through the gates into the city.

"For without are dogs, and sorcerers, and whoremongers, and murderers, and idolaters, and whosoever loveth and maketh a lie."

Nor does the Bible tell us, or any where intimate, that these latter will *ever* enter into the blessedness of eternal life. But all who thirst for and are willing to take of its waters, may enter in. Therefore it is written again : "Let him that is athirst, come. And whosoever will, let him take the water of life freely."

But Swedenborg has himself told us *why* a man's ruling love cannot be changed after death ; and why, therefore, the hells must be unending in their duration. It may be alike interesting and instructive to consider some of his reasons, which I shall proceed to do in the next chapter.

9

VIII.

THE doctrine revealed for the New Church—revealed
so clearly, too, that there is no ground for a difference of opinion on this subject—is, that the love
which rules supreme in the heart of man at the time of
or previous to his death, will forever remain unchanged
in its nature. Very often does the illumined herald of
the New Church declare, that, "As man is when he dies,
such he remains to eternity." "The life of a man cannot
be changed after the body dies." "If evil is not removed
[from the soul] in the world, it cannot be removed afterward." "The life which a man contracts [or forms for
himself] in the world, remains with him for ever."
"To change the ruling love in a spirit, would be to deprive him of his life, or to annihilate him." "No one's
life can possibly be changed after death." "Evil life
can by no means be changed [after death] into good life,
nor infernal life into angelic." "The angels declare
that it were easier to change a bat into a dove, or an
owl into a bird of paradise, than an infernal spirit into

112

an angel of heaven." "Infernal love can never be changed into heavenly love [after death]. . . . This is what is meant by the words of Abraham addressed to the rich man in hell : 'Between us and you there is a great gulf fixed,'" etc. "Hence it is evident that all who go to hell, remain there for ever."

In such clear and explicit declarations on this subject, do the writings of Swedenborg abound. If then, we accept his teachings concerning the future life, as a divinely authorized revelation of the solemn realities of the spiritual world, we must believe that a person's ruling love cannot be changed after death ; and therefore that the condition and character of the wicked in the Hereafter, will remain essentially the same to all eternity.

And we cannot reject this doctrine, or set up another in its place, viz. this :—that all who pass into the other world in an infernal or supremely selfish state, will ultimately be brought out of that state and become shining angels—without undermining or deranging the entire system of Swedenborg's spiritual philosophy. To be consistent, we must set aside his doctrine of degrees ; his doctrine concerning the nature of the final judgment; his doctrine of human freedom and the law of moral growth ; his doctrine of spiritual equilibrium ; together with his great law of spiritual affinity which determines all associations in the spiritual world. So intimately are all truths linked or dovetailed together, that it is no easy matter to remove one, or substitute a falsity in its place,

10 *   H

without disturbing the entire system of which that truth makes a part.

The great Swede's doctrine on this subject, then, has the merit of perfect consistency; while any different doctrine is seen, upon slight examination, to be in direct conflict with other facts and laws announced by him, the obvious truth and rationality of which compel the assent of intelligent and candid minds.

But not only has Swedenborg declared the fact that a man's ruling love cannot be changed after death, but he has told us *why* it cannot. In proclaiming the endless duration of the hells, he has at the same time given us the philosophical reason. It is, that when the ruling love is fully unfolded, and everything that disagrees with it is rejected, hated, loathed, the individual is then precisely what this love makes him from centre to circumference. If it be the love of self, then he is selfish all through; just as a crocodile is a crocodile, a wolf a wolf, or a serpent a serpent all through. And he has no more desire to change that love, or to receive an unselfish, heavenly love in lieu of it, or to become any other than the supremely selfish being that he is, than a wolf has to become a sheep, or a serpent a dove. And without the *desire* to overcome the love of self, and to have the opposite heavenly love implanted or developed in the soul, can we conceive it possible that this change will ever take place? Human character in this world or in the world to come, is not, as I have before remarked, developed under the law of vegetable growth. Its formation everywhere implies the exercise of human volition, and never takes place without it. A vegetable germ unfolds into a plant or tree according to an implanted instinct or law of its nature, and without volition. But is there any human germ, hidden away in the inmosts or elsewhere of the human spirit,—*can* there be any—that will ever develop into true manhood or womanhood in like manner?—that is, without conscious volition on the part of the individual? And if the properly human or heavenly growth can never take place without volition, how can the needed volition spring up in the soul of one who has passed the ordeal of judgment, and become thoroughly and supremely selfish?

True, there is but one life; and all life in derivative forms, is one and the same in its origin. The same exhaustless Fountain that vitalizes the organism of the sheep, supplies the wolf also with life. The form into which the life flows, makes all the difference in its quality or manifestations. And we cannot conceive how a wolf could be changed into a sheep, without such a complete change in its entire organism, as would utterly destroy its identity. And this destroyed, where is the original wolf? Annihilated, beyond question.

Let us hear, now, the reasons which Swedenborg himself has given, showing *why* a man's ruling love cannot be changed after death. He says:

"I have also heard from the angels that no one's life

can be changed after death, because it is organized according to his love and faith, and hence according to his works; and that if the life were changed, the organization would be destroyed, which can never be done. They further added, that a change of organization can only take place in the material body, and by no means in the spiritual body after the former has been rejected." (*Brief Exposition* n. 110; *Conjugial Love* 524.)

"I have been told by the angels that [after death] the life of the ruling love is never changed with any one, since every one is his own love; wherefore to change that love in a spirit, would be to deprive him of his life, or to annihilate him. They also stated the reason, which is, that man after death is no longer capable of being reformed by instruction as in the world, because the ultimate plane which consists of natural knowledges and affections, is then quiescent, and cannot be opened because it is not spiritual; that the interiors which belong to the rational and natural mind, rest upon that plane like a house on its foundation; and that it is for this reason that a man remains for ever such as the life of his love had been in the world." (*Heaven and Hell* n. 480.)

"By washing the feet is meant to purify the natural principle of man; for unless this principle in man be purified and cleansed when he lives in the world, it cannot afterward be purified to eternity; for such as his natural principle is when he dies, such it remains; nor is it afterward amended, since it is that plane into which interior things which are spiritual flow, it being their receptacle; therefore when this is perverted, interior things when they flow in, are perverted in like manner. The case herein is as when the eye is injured, or any other organ of sense or member of the body; on which occasion interior things feel and act by them no otherwise than according to reception therein. Therefore it is that man can never be purified to eternity if he be not purified as to his natural principle in the world; this is meant by the Lord's words, 'What I do thou knowest not now, but thou shalt know hereafter.'" (*Arcana Cœlestia* 10,243.)

Then there are *degrees* belonging to the mind; and the influx of life is through the higher degrees to the lower; and the quality of the life that inflows, or the character of the individual, is according to the form of the natural degree which receives the influx. If this degree is in a disordered or hellish form, it changes God's love and wisdom as they flow in, into their opposites; comparatively as the fox-glove or deadly nightshade changes the sunshine and the rain and the sweet dews of heaven into poison. But if this degree be regenerated or restored to order, then the whole man is regenerated. Life being received into an orderly natural form, is felt and manifested as the true life.

The character, therefore, of the lower or natural degree of a man's mind, since it determines for ever the quality

of the life that inflows, must necessarily determine for
ever the character of the man. The interior life is terminated in, and therefore takes on the character of, the
external or natural life, just as the light and heat of the
sun, terminating in hideous forms and excrementitious
substances, take on the ugliness of the one and the offen-
siveness of the other. Accordingly Swedenborg says:

"A man's interiors are distinguished into degrees, and
in every degree are terminated, and by termination separated each from the interior degree; and this from the
inmost to the outermost. . . . These degrees in man
are most distinct; hence, if he lives in good, he is as to
his interiors a heaven in its least form, or his interiors
correspond to the three heavens. And therefore if a
man has lived the life of charity and love, he can after
death be translated even into the third heaven: but in
order to acquire such a capacity, it is necessary that all
his degrees be well terminated, and thus by terminations
be distinct from each other; and when they are terminated, or by terminations are made distinct, every degree
is a plane in which the good inflowing from the Lord
rests and is received. Without these degrees as planes
good cannot be received but flows through, as through
a sieve or a perforated basket, even to the sensual [plane],
and in that is changed to what is filthy, viz., into the
delight of self-love and the love of the world, conse-
quently into the delight of hatred, revenge, cruelty, adultery, avarice, or into mere voluptuousness and luxurious-

ness, which delight appears to those who are in it as good. . . .

" In the other life especially it is discovered whether the things of a man's will have been terminated or not. With those in whom they have been terminated, there is a zeal for spiritual good and truth, or for what is just and right; for they had done good for the sake of good and truth, and had acted justly for the sake of what is just and right, not for the sake of gain, honor, and the like. All those with whom the interiors of the will have been terminated, are elevated to heaven, for the influent Divine can lead them ; but all those with whom the interiors of the will have not been terminated, betake themselves to hell, for the Divine flows through and is turned into what is infernal, as in the case of the sun's heat, which falling upon filthy excrements, produces a foul stench." (*Arcana Cœlestia* 5145.)

" With things relating to spiritual birth, the case is such that reception must be altogether in the natural principle. This is why, during man's regeneration, the natural principle is first prepared to receive ; and so far as this principle is rendered capable of receiving, so far interior goods and truths can be brought forth and multiplied. For this reason also, if the natural man be not prepared to receive the truths and goods of faith in the life of the body, he cannot receive them in the other life, and therefore cannot be saved. This is what is meant by the expression so often used, that, as the tree

falls, so it lies ; or, as a man dies, so his state remains.
For man has with him in the other life all the natural
memory, or the memory of the external man, but is not
permitted to use it in that life ; wherefore it is there as a
fundamental plane into which interior truths and goods
fall ; and if that plane is incapable of receiving the truths
and goods which flow in from an interior principle, they
are either extinguished, perverted or rejected." (Ibid.
4588.)

These degrees of the mind, Swedenborg tells us, exist
in every man, "from his birth potentially, and actually
when opened." And he tells us, also, how the higher
or heavenly degrees of life are opened ; and that every
one after death, "enters that degree which was opened
within him in the world." (*Divine Love and Wisdom*
238.) But evil, or the indulgence of a supremely selfish
and worldly love by the natural mind, closes more and
more firmly the higher or heavenly degrees.

"In such a man—[one who 'delights in all kinds of
wickedness, as in adultery, fraud, revenge, blasphemy,
and so on']—the spiritual mind is more and more
firmly closed ; the confirmation of the evil by the false
especially closes it. Therefore evil and the false once
confirmed, cannot be extirpated after death ; this can
only be done in the world by repentance." (Ibid. 262.)

I have quoted freely that the reader may see the reasons given by Swedenborg himself, why a man's ruling
love cannot be changed after death ; and why, therefore,

the hells must be eternal in .duration. And they are reasons, we observe, growing out of, harmonizing with, and making indeed a part of, his grand and comprehensive system of spiritual philosophy. So that, in adopting a different view from the one he has taught in regard to the duration of the hells—in denying their eternity, and insisting that, some time or other and in some way or other, the ruling love *will* be changed after death, and the devils be all converted into angels—we not only reject a doctrine as clearly revealed as anything can be, but we are compelled also to sweep away so much of his spiritual philosophy as would leave his whole system tottering. We are compelled to *deny* that the life's love can become so inwrought into the spiritual organism during one's earthly pilgrimage, that an entire change in the quality of the love would involve annihilation, or a total destruction of the soul's organism (C. L. 524; H. H. 480). We are compelled to deny, what we are repeatedly assured the angels affirm, that the interior things of the mind, resting for ever on the ultimate or natural plane of life developed here on earth "like a house on its foundation," will for ever be in harmony or correspondence with that plane. (Ibid.) We must deny, too, that there is any such eternal and indissoluble connection between the life here and the life hereafter, as Swedenborg has declared; or that any such cleansing of the external or natural man here below as he alleges, is essential to that internal purification without which there

11

can be no heaven. (A. C. 10,243.) We must deny the
declared existence of degrees to the mind ; or that no
higher degree of life can be entered and enjoyed in the
other world, than the degree which has been opened in
this. We must deny that the lower or natural degree
bears any such fixed and permanent relation to the
higher, as the eye bears to seeing or the ear to hearing.
And considerably more must we deny, if we would be
consistent.

Who that has studied Swedenborg enough to grasp a
tithe of his deep and comprehensive philosophy, and
has felt constrained by the illuminating power of his
writings to acknowledge that he was, indeed, a man or-
dained and sent of God, dares venture on such a string
of denials? Yet they all follow inevitably from the denial of his doctrine concerning the eternity of the hells,
or the assumption that a man's ruling love *may* be
changed after death.

Then apply to the doctrine taught by Swedenborg on
this subject one other test—that most searching one
of all—that divinely authorized touch-stone of truth and
of error expressed in the formula, "By their fruits ye
shall know them."

Judge the doctrine by its fruits—that is, by its obvious
influence on the character of believers. Compare it
in this respect with that other doctrine which some
would substitute in its place—viz., the doctrine that
a man may repent and his ruling love be changed in

the other world, and the devils be ultimately all converted into angels.

The New Church doctrine says: "Keep the commandments; shun evils as sins; deny self, take up the cross and follow the Lord. For if you do not, while on earth, *begin* the great work of building up the kingdom of heaven in your heart, you will have no inclination to begin this work beyond the grave; and that blessed kingdom will, therefore, never be yours."

The other doctrine, stripped of its fine rhetoric and speaking in the plainest language, says: "It is best, of course, to keep the commandments. This will carry you to heaven quickest. But live as you will—sin as you may—trample on all the laws of God as you choose—indulge your avarice, your lust, your pride, your selfishness, your hate, to any excess—develop and strengthen within you the life of hell to whatever extent—and God will some day, spite of yourself and every other obstacle, bring you out of that hellish state, and make you a shining and happy angel."

Now which of these doctrines is it best for men to believe? Which is most stimulating to the better part of our nature, and most helpful in repressing and restraining the worse? Which is most likely to excite to prayer and watchfulness? to patience and self-denial and holy endeavor? to inward and persevering conflict with the foes of our own household? Which is the most wholesome doctrine to preach?—which the most benign

in its practical tendency and effects? It is not difficult,
I think, to answer these questions. And let us remember
that "a good tree cannot bring forth evil fruit, neither
can a corrupt tree bring forth good fruit." Nor is it
possible for a false doctrine to exert upon the hearts and
lives of men a more benign influence than the truth.

IX.

DISPLAYS OF THE DIVINE BENIGNITY IN HELL.

M AN alone, of all created beings, is endowed with
Liberty and Rationality. These are the properly
human faculties. Without them *he would not be man.*
These are the faculties which alone render him morally
accountable. Without them, he would have been incapable of either sin or holiness; and to have been incapable of these, he must have been something other than
man—a very different being from what he is.

Why is not the wolf or the bear morally responsible?
Why is every other creature incapable of sin? Simply
because man alone is endowed with what belongs to no
other creature—a moral sense—the power to discrimi-
nate and the liberty to choose between justice and injus-
tice, right and wrong; or in other words, with the
faculties of rationality and liberty, which alone distin-
guish him from the brute creation and make him man.

But the very possession of these faculties involves a
responsibility corresponding in magnitude to the dignity
and worth of the endowment. It involves, moreover,
the liability of their abuse and utter perversion by the

11 *   125

possessor, and the possibility, therefore, of a spiritual
lapse. And this must have been foreseen by the great
Giver of these faculties. And now comes the question:

What shall be done with a man when he fails to dis
charge the obligations which the gift bestowed on him
imposes?—when he abuses his properly human faculties,
and yields to the promptings of his lower, carnal, animal
nature, regardless of his obligations as a morally accountable being? What provision should infinite Love
and Wisdom make for those who violate, and persist in
violating, the laws of their spiritual or properly *human*
nature? To say that their condition will be the same and
their happiness the same in the Hereafter, as if they had
faithfully obeyed these laws, is to utter what every enlightened mind sees to be absurd. As reasonably might
one maintain that no penalty ought to be attached to the
violation of physical laws; that men ought to be permitted to eat arsenic without being poisoned; to handle
red hot iron without being burned; to leap from the top
of Bunker Hill monument without being bruised; or to
stick their bodies full of pins without suffering pain.
There is everywhere and always a penalty attached to the
violation of law. This is both wise and right. Otherwise laws would be without meaning and without force.

But infinite Love must make the best possible provision
which infinite Wisdom can suggest, for those who abuse
their human faculties, and obstinately persist in violating
the laws of their spiritual being. It is bound *by its very*

nature to do this. And who can doubt that it will do it? The illumined Swedenborg assures us that it actually does do it; and he tells us how. Nothing can exceed the extent and beauty of the Divine beneficence, as displayed in the provision made for those in the other world, who, by a life of evil here on earth, have confirmed themselves in a state of opposition to the Divine, and to the laws of their own inner and heavenly life.

"Life is love," is a remark often made by Swedenborg. And a man's ruling love is his life. His character is according to the nature of this love;—pure and heavenly if the love be pure; vile and infernal if the love be selfish. The ruling love is the inner and ever active force, perpetually working to mould the whole outer man—his words, tones, looks and actions—into perfect correspondence with itself.

Look at the face of an inveterate miser. How visibly is the spirit that prompts and sways him imprinted there! Or that of the confirmed inebriate—is it not the very image of bestiality? Or listen to the tones of the hard-hearted, cruel and malignant—are they not in perfect agreement with the affections from which they proceed? So with hate, revenge, jealousy, despair—every strong passion or deep feeling long indulged—its manifest tendency is to mould the countenance and the whole outer man into perfect correspondence with itself. And on the other hand who has not seen the very beauty, brightness and joy of heaven beaming from the face of one in whose heart love to the Lord and the neighbor has long been the ruling principle of action?

Now under the operation of this law—a law too generally recognized and too long established to be for a moment called in question—what ought to be the appearance of evil spirits in the other world, where infernal loves have taken full possession of their souls, from centre to circumference? Why, they ought to be monsters in form as they are in feeling and purpose. Their looks and tones ought to be the true expression of the infernal loves that rule them. Accordingly Swedenborg says:

"All the spirits in the hells, when inspected in any degree of heavenly light, appear in the form of their own evil; for every one there is the effigy of his own evil, because with every one the interiors and exteriors act in unity,—the interiors exhibiting themselves visibly in the exteriors, which are the face, the body, the speech, and the gestures. Thus their quality is known as soon as they are seen. In general, they are forms of contempt of others; of menace against those who do not pay them respect; of hatred of various kinds; also of various kinds of revenge. Ferocity and cruelty from their interiors are transparent through those forms. But when others commend, honor, and worship them, their faces are contracted, and have an appearance of gladness arising from delight. It is impossible to describe in a few words all those forms, as they actually appear, for no one of them is similar to another. Among those, how-

ever, who are in a similar evil, and thence in a similar
infernal society, there is a general likeness, from which,
as from a plane of derivation, the faces of all there
appear to bear a certain resemblance to each other. In
general, their faces are hideous, and void of life like
corpses; in some cases they are black; in others they
are fiery like little torches; in others, disfigured with
pimples, warts, and ulcers. . . . Their bodies also are
monstrous; and their speech is like the speech of anger,
hatred, or revenge,—for every one speaks from his own
falsity, and in a tone corresponding to his own evil. In
a word, they are all images of their own hell."—*Heaven
and Hell*, n. 553.

And mark here the unspeakable love and mercy of the
Lord!—the wonderful display of the Divine benignity!
The devils are not permitted to see themselves or each
other as the hideous creatures they really are. They
only appear under these disgusting and loathsome forms
when seen, as Swedenborg saw them, in the light of
heaven; for this light alone reveals the real quality of
persons and things. Seen in the false and fatuous glare
of hell, nothing appears as it really is. And so the true
character of the devils—their internal and external deformity—is mercifully concealed from themselves and
from each other. Their dreadful wickedness does not
seem *to them* wickedness, but praiseworthy shrewdness.
Their unmitigated foolishness seems *to them* not foolishness at all, but rarest wisdom. They do not appear to

each other like the horrid monsters they are, but like a
very respectable class of people. In their own light, and
to each other's eyes, they look not hideous but quite
human. Their bitter and fiendish tones have in them
nothing harsh or grating to each other's ears; on the
contrary they seem quite agreeable and even musical to
them. Accordingly Swedenborg, after describing the
loathsome appearance of the devils as seen by himself in
the clear light of heaven, adds:

"It is, however, to be observed, that such is the appearance of infernal spirits when seen in the light of
heaven; but among themselves they appear like men.
This is of the Lord's mercy, that they may not appear as
loathsome to each other as they do to the angels. But
this appearance is a fallacy; for as soon as a ray of light
from heaven is let in, their human forms are turned into
monstrous ones, such as they are in reality, as described
above; for in the light of heaven everything appears as it
really is."—Ibid.

Again he says:

"Among the wonderful things which exist in the other
life, this also is one: that, when the angels of heaven
look into evil spirits, these latter have a totally different
appearance from what they have when seen among themselves. Among themselves and in their own fatuous
light, which is like that of a coal fire, as before remarked, they appear to themselves in a human form, and
also, according to their fantasies, not without beauty;

but when the same spirits are looked into by the angels of heaven, that light is instantly dissipated, and they appear with entirely different faces, each according to his character; some dusky and black as devils; some with pale ghastly faces like corpses;—some like skeletons; and, more wonderful still, some like monsters, the deceitful like serpents, and the most deceitful like vipers; and others in other forms. But as soon as the angels remove their sight from them, they appear in their above mentioned forms, which they have when seen in their own light."—*Arcana Cœlestia* n. 4533. See also A. C. 4798.—H. H. 481.

A wonderful display, indeed, is it of the Lord's unspeakable love and mercy, that He does not permit infernal spirits to see themselves or one another as they really are!

And we have similar illustrations of the Divine benignity here on earth. The desperately wicked never see their own moral deformity. Their eyes are blinded out of tenderest mercy toward them; for to see themselves as they appear in the light of heaven, would cause them unutterable agony. Take any class of the most hardened villains you can find—those of a character nearest allied to that of devils, such as gamblers, thieves, swindlers, murderers, fornicators, pimps, pirates—does any one imagine that these people see themselves to be the dreadful creatures they really are? Have they any idea of their terrible moral deformity? Not one of

them, in their ordinary evil state. How can they? for
they are not in the all-revealing light of heaven, but in
the fatuous light of hell; and this light which is real
darkness, forever blinds and bewilders. In their own
infernal light, these fellows appear to each other very
respectable—appear, indeed, like men; but in the light
of the Divine Word, or as viewed by heavenly minded
people, they appear not as *men* but as *monsters*.

And not only are the faces and the whole personal appearance of the devils in exact correspondence with their
evil loves, but all their surroundings exist under the
very same law, and are produced in the same way. All
the objects they look upon are but the embodied forms
of their own evil loves. So that their whole outward or
phenomenal world is a perfect reflection, under the law
of correspondence, of their internal or spiritual condition.

Accordingly we are told that the devils appear clad in
filthy and tattered garments; that they dwell in deserts,
bogs, and miry places—some of them in caves and dens
like those of wild beasts; that among the objects by which
they are surrounded, are dreary deserts, rocky and barren
wastes, thorns and thistles, ferocious beasts and venom-
ous reptiles, dirty pools and heaps of filth. And these
things (all of which are spiritual in their nature) are but
the embodied forms, under the law of correspondence,
of the filthy and infernal loves of the evil spirits themselves. To quote again from Swedenborg:

" How the delights of every one's life are turned into corresponding delights after death, may indeed be known from the science of correspondences; but because that science is not yet generally known, I will illustrate the subject by some examples from experience.

" All those who are in evil, and have confirmed themselves in falsities against the truths of the church, and especially those who have rejected the Word, shun the light of heaven, and betake themselves to subterranean places, which through the openings appear very dark, and to the clefts of rocks, and there hide themselves. And they seek such retreats because they have loved falsities and hated truths; for such caverns, and clefts of rocks, and darkness also, correspond to falsities, and light corresponds to truth. It is their delight to dwell in such places, and undelightful to them to dwell in open plains.

" In like manner do those who have taken delight in clandestine and insidious plots, and in the secret contrivance of fraudulent schemes; these, too, are in those caverns, and enter into chambers so dark that they cannot even see one another, and there they whisper in each other's ears in corners. This is what the delight of their love is turned into.

" They who have studied the sciences with no other end than to acquire the reputation of learning, and who have not cultivated their rational faculty by means of them, and have taken delight in the things of memory

12

from pride thence derived, love sandy places, which they choose in preference to fields and gardens, because sandy places correspond to such studies.

"They who have been acquainted with the doctrinals of their own church and of others, and have not applied any of their knowledge to life, choose for themselves rocky places, and dwell among heaps of stones, shunning places that are cultivated, because they dislike them.

"They who have ascribed all things to nature, and they also who have ascribed all things to their own prudence, and who by various artifices have raised themselves to honors, and have acquired wealth, apply themselves in the other life to the study of magical arts, which are abuses of divine order, and find therein the highest delight of their life. They who have applied divine truths to gratify their own loves, and thus have falsified them, love urinous places and odors, because these correspond to the delights of such love.

"They who have been sordidly avaricious, dwell in huts, and love swinish filth, and such nidorous exhalations as proceed from indigested substances in the stomach. They who have passed their life in mere pleasures, have lived delicately, and indulged their appetites, prizing such enjoyments as the highest good of life, love excrementitious things and privies in the other life. These are delightful to them, because such pleasures are spiritual filth. They shun places that are clean and free from dirt, because such places are undelightful to them."

Here, again, we are called to admire the unspeakable love and mercy of the Lord as manifested toward those in the other world who are "enemies to him by wicked works." For we must remember that all the objects which greet their senses—though *in reality* just as Swedenborg has described them—appear very different to the devils from what they did to him, or from what they do to our imagination—for *we* are able to contemplate them in some degree of heavenly light. The regions they inhabit are certainly dismal enough; but not dismal *to them*. All the objects by which they are surrounded, are really hideous and loathsome to angelic natures; but not hideous or loathsome *to them*. The odors they inhale, so fetid and offensive to angels, are by no means offensive *to them*. On the contrary the devils find these things quite agreeable and even delightful; for they accord perfectly with their nature; they agree with their desires or loves; they are in exact correspondence with their life.

Everywhere and always life seeks that which is in agreement with its nature. Nothing else will satisfy its cravings. Such is the nature of the devils, that the scenery of hell, so dismal and repulsive to our imagination, is quite agreeable *to them;*—more beautiful, indeed, to their eyes than would be the splendors and magnificence of heaven. Their life being what it is—degraded, bestial, infernal—the objects that surround them are the very ones with which *they* are best pleased; for they suit their tastes, being in perfect correspondence with their life. *To them,* their dens and caverns seem preferable to the most gorgeous palaces of heaven ; their filthy rags more seemly than the shining. garments of the angels ; their fetid stenches more grateful to *their* nostrils than would be the sweetest perfume from the gardens of the blest. "It is *delightful* to the devils," says Swedenborg, "to inhabit such places [as caverns and clefts of the rocks], and *un*delightful to them to dwell in open fields." "They *love* sandy places, and prefer them to fields and gardens." "They *love* mean and squalid brothels." "They *love* the filth of swine." "They *love* urinous places and scents, because these things correspond to the delights of their life."

I am aware that this will sound very strange to minds much confirmed in the old ideas. It will seem to them utterly incredible that such unsightly and disgusting objects as those above mentioned, should be delightful to the devils. But they will see upon reflection that nothing could be more reasonable. For are there not animals that delight in just such sights and smells here on earth ? If so, then these things are agreeable to *some* kinds of life. They are in perfect correspondence with *some* natures, as truly so as beautiful gardens and the perfume of sweetest flowers are in correspondence with the nature of angels. To crows and kites the smell of carrion is not unpleasant, but delightful. Owls and bats prefer darkness to light. Mire and filth are not unsightly, but beautiful to the eyes of swine ; and the stench of their own stye is quite agreeable to their nostrils. Serpents and vipers love the clefts of rocks; foxes love deserts; rats prefer cellars and subterranean regions; turtles and crocodiles seek marshy places; and to the eyes of wolves and bears their own dens, undoubtedly, seem more beautiful and home-like than would the palaces of kings.

Who cannot see that the things which such creatures prefer for food, the odors they delight to inhale, and the places they love to inhabit, affect their senses in a manner very different from what they do ours? And the only reason to be assigned is, that their life is very different from the properly human. Their loves and consequent tastes are different from ours. And they choose and delight in what is agreeable to *their* life, as we do what is agreeable to ours. Says Swedenborg:

"The delights belonging to the lusts of evil, and those belonging to affections for the good, cannot be compared; because resident within the former is the devil, and within the latter is the Lord. If a comparison must be drawn, the delights of the lusts of evil can only be compared to the lasciviousness of frogs in ponds, and of serpents in slimy places; while the delights of affections for the good may be compared to mental delights in gardens and flowers. For things similar to those which are pleasing to frogs and serpents, are also pleasing to those in the hells who are in the lusts of evil; and things similar to those which are pleasing to the mind in gardens and flowers, are also pleasing to those in the

12 *

heavens who are in affections for the good. For as before stated, unclean correspondences are pleasing to the evil, and clean correspondences to the good."—*Divine Providence* n. 40.

And are there not, even in this world, people who seem to prefer disorder, filth and squalor, to order, neatness and cleanliness? Have you never seen persons, who, if they were presented with the most magnificent habitation, filled and surrounded, too, with everything beautiful, and arranged in the most orderly and tasteful manner, would, if left to do precisely as they pleased, convert that palatial residence into a vile and loathsome place in less than six months? Are there not some whose nature (inherited, or acquired by habit,) is so near akin to that of certain animals, that they would very soon convert the sweetest and most lovely place of abode, into a squalid and disgusting stye? Their nature is such that cleanliness and order seem far less agreeable to them, than filth and disorder. And, place them where you will, they will very soon reduce all their surroundings to a condition that will reveal with great clearness the state of their own minds. So on the other hand, place people of refinement and culture in the humblest cabin, and they will soon make that cabin reveal to the careful observer something of their refined and cultivated tastes. And the reason of this is, that every kind of life is delighted with, and therefore seeks, that which corresponds with its own nature.

But it does not appear after all, some may say, how the devils, having once been men in the natural world, can find delight in things which here on earth are known to be agreeable only to a low order of animals.

It does not? Let the reader reflect for a moment. What has made those people devils? What kind of life is theirs?—the life, too, that they have freely chosen? It is not angelic life. It is not properly human. It is the life of self and sense—mere corporeal or animal, not celestial life. They have marred and spoiled their truly human life; or have suffered it to become stifled and overrun by a rank luxuriance of thorns and thistles and noxious weeds, which, if not carefully and betimes rooted out, are sure to spring up and take possession of the natural heart. Only a kind of bestial life, therefore, is left them—such life as corresponds to, and forms the very essence of, animals like those above mentioned. This life, therefore, *must* from its very nature, seek and find delight in scenes and objects which are agreeable to such animals.

Considering the nature of the devils, therefore, or the kind of life they have freely chosen and made their own, it is most reasonable that the hideous and loathsome objects by which they are surrounded, should not appear hideous or loathsome *to them*, but pleasant and altogether agreeable; for they are all in perfect correspondence with their life's love. And whatever corresponds to this, is always perceived as delightful.

But if this be really so, some will say, what is there, after all, to choose between heaven and hell? What great advantage has one over the other? The devils, you say, have their delights as well as the angels, though they are not delighted with precisely the same things. They have what is most agreeable to their nature. Their surroundings as well as their associates are such as *they* prefer. They go in freedom where they wish to go—into the society of congenial spirits; and there they feel quite at home. What great inducement is there, then, to strive for heaven, or to shun hell?

It is true that every kind of love has its delights. But the nature of the delight is according to the quality of the love. The purer the love, the more exalted the delight. The delights of the devils, therefore, as compared with those of the angels, are as the delights of bears and crocodiles compared with those of Christ-like men; yea, they are as the sweetness and tranquillity of love, compared with the bitterness and unrest of hatred.

Why is God so unspeakably happy—the happiest Being in the universe? Because He is the best. Because his love is the purest. It is the love of others out of Himself—the love of imparting happiness. And the more a man grows to be like God—the more he receives of His unselfish love, the more does he enjoy of that sweet peace which it is in the very nature of this love to bestow. While the less of this love he receives—the more selfish and *un*-like the Lord he is, the more does he experience of that inward unrest which it is the nature of this opposite love to produce.

Who that has ever truly loved—be it husband, mother,
wife or child—does not know that in the exercise of disinterested love, there is an unspeakable bliss which the
world cannot give? The Lord promises peace—his own
peace—to all who humbly acknowledge Him, and willingly consecrate themselves on the altar of duty.
"Peace I leave with you," says He to all such—"my
peace I give unto you." There is true peace nowhere
but in Him;—nowhere but in the reception and exercise
of his unselfish love. Therefore He says: "In me ye
shall have peace." And when those who have followed
Him in the regeneration, enter the spiritual world and
come more fully into their life's love, they will receive
in greater fullness than ever before the delights of that
love. They will then know, from the sweet seraphic
joy that floods their souls, the full meaning of the words,
"Enter thou into the joy of thy Lord."

But they who have yielded habitually to the promptings of their lower nature, regardless of God and the
good of the neighbor, and have not denied self, taken
up the cross, and followed the Divine Master—these,
when they enter the other world, come more fully into
the life and delights of self-love. And what are these?
The delights of fraud, hatred, revenge, adultery, blasphemy, wickedness of every kind;—delights, indeed, to
those whose ruling love is the love of self, but torment

and unmitigated misery when compared with the pure ecstatic delights of angelic love. Therefore these persons are represented as receiving the sentence, "Depart from me, into everlasting fire prepared for the devil and his angels."

The truth, then, summarily stated, is: that all life, from that of the highest angel in heaven down to that of the meanest creature here on earth, has its delights; for life is love, and all love has its delights. The degree of happiness which each creature enjoys, depends upon the character of his delights; and the character or exaltation of his delights, depends on the nature or quality of his love. And as far as the human transcends in dignity the bestial life—as far as man surpasses the brute in wisdom or in the extent and variety of his powers, so far has he the capacity of enjoyment above (yes, and of misery *below*) that of the brutes, and so far does the happiness of the angels exceed that of the devils.

Is not this new view of hell in the highest degree rational? What can be more reasonable, (in view of the kind of life which infernal spirits have voluntarily made their own) than that they should be totally oblivious of their own condition?—that they should be unable to see themselves or one another or the objects that surround them, as they really are?—that everything should seem to them quite different from what it is, and from what it actually appears when viewed in the light of heaven?—that they should remain forever ignorant of *realities*, and spend an eternity in the midst of shadows and phantasms? (See *Arcana Cœlestia* 4623.)

And what unspeakable benignity in our Heavenly Father, does this doctrine display! When his children have wandered far from the way of his commandments; when they have shut their souls against the light of his wisdom and the purity of his love, and confirmed themselves in a life of evil; He loves them still—loves them too tenderly to permit them to see where and what they are. He loves them, and, for their own good, mercifully provides that they remain forever oblivious of what they were created to be; that they shall not be permitted to see themselves or each other as monsters, but as men; that the loathsome objects which surround them, and which their own evil loves create by an unfailing law, shall not seem loathsome but pleasing to them; that they shall still enjoy what *they* call delights—delights, too, as elevated as the kind of life they have formed for themselves, will possibly admit of.

Where shall we find a more striking display of the Lord's infinite and unspeakable mercy, than is presented in the wonderful provision He has made for the comfort and highest welfare of the devils? His love is, indeed, unfathomable. "His mercy is forever." Who can unfold his marvelous loving-kindness? "Who can show forth all his praise?"

"The Lord is good to *all*, and his tender mercies are over all his works."

"Whither shall I go from thy Spirit? or whither shall I flee from thy presence? If I ascend up into heaven, thou art there; if I make my bed in hell, behold, thou art there."

"Ye have heard that it hath been said, Thou shalt love thy neighbor and hate thine enemy.

"But I say unto you, Love your enemies, bless them that curse you, do good to them that hate you, and pray for them which despitefully use you and persecute you;

"That ye may be the children of your Father which is in heaven: for He maketh his sun to rise on the evil and on the good, and sendeth rain on the just and on the unjust."

X.

SWEDENBORG has disclosed with great clearness the condition of the wicked in the other world. Nor does he pretend to give us merely his *opinion* on the subject, but to set forth what he actually heard and saw when his spiritual senses were opened. He has told us what sort of people he found in hell, or of whom it consists. To cite his own language:

"Hell consists of spirits who, while living in the world, denied God, acknowledged nature, lived contrary to divine order, loved evils and falsities (although not so much before the world on account of the appearance) and who, therefore, were either insane in regard to truths, or despised and denied them, if not with the mouth, yet in heart [and in their lives]. Of all such, who have lived from the creation of the world, hell consists."— *Athanasian Creed* n. 41.

The wickedness of the infernals is described as terrible —surpassing all belief. Speaking of their "malignity, cunning, fraud, deceit, and cruelty," he says:

"These are such and so great that, if they were told

only in part, scarcely an individual in the world would believe it. The infernals are so cunning and artful, and likewise so wicked—in short they are of such a character, that they cannot possibly be resisted by any man, nor even by any angel, but by the Lord alone"—A.C. 6666. And speaking of those who have lived wicked lives on earth, and have interiorly denied the Divine, he says: "Such persons in the other life, when they come into the state of their interiors, and are heard to speak and seen to act, appear as if infatuated; for from their evil lusts they break out into all manner of abominations—into contempt of others, ridicule, blasphemy, hatred and revenge. They contrive plans of mischief, some of them with such cunning and malice, that it can scarcely be believed that anything of the kind could exist in any man." "They lay snares; they cherish hatred; they burn with revenge, and seek to vent their rage against all who do not submit themselves to them. . . . At last they deliberate with themselves how they may climb up into heaven so as to destroy that, or be worshiped there as gods. To such lengths does their madness go. Those of this class who have been of the Roman Catholic religion, are more insane than the rest." "[When on earth] they desired to be worshiped as gods, and therefore burned with hatred and revenge against all who did not acknowledge their power over the souls of men and over heaven. They still cherished the same disposition which distinguished them in the world, that is, the same hatred and revenge against those who oppose them. Their greatest delight is to exercise cruelty; but this delight is turned against themselves; for in their hells one rages like a madman against another who derogates from his divine power." And, as might be expected, "within their habitations, they are engaged in continual quarrels, enmities, blows and fightings, while in the streets and lanes of their cities are robberies and depredations"—*Heaven and Hell* 506, '8, 86.

Such is the sad condition in the great Hereafter of those who, while on earth, have disregarded and trampled on the laws of their spiritual and heavenly life, and have thereby brought themselves into a state to love darkness rather than light, and evil rather than good. And the ruling love, we are told, can never be changed in the other world.

Swedenborg has told us of various kinds of hells which he was permitted to inspect *—for no two of the infernal societies are precisely alike; and their punishments are

---

* In order that he might learn the actual state of things in hell, from his own personal observation, he says: "I was sometimes let down thither. To be let down into hell, is not to be translated from one *place* to another; but it is an immission into some infernal society, while the person remains in the same place." On one of these occasions, he continues, "I clearly perceived that a kind of column, as it were, encompassed me, which became sensibly stronger; and I perceived also that this was the wall of brass spoken of in the Word, formed of angelic spirits, in order that I might be let down in safety among the unhappy."—*Arcana Cœlestia* 699.

as various as their characters, but admirably adapted to
their states and needs.   Thus he speaks of "the hells of
those who have spent their lives in hatred, revenge, and
cruelty;" of "the hells of those who have lived in adultery and lasciviousness;" of "the hells of the deceitful;" of "the hells of the covetous and of robbers;" of
"the hells of those who have lived in merely carnal
pleasures," etc.   And while the ruling spirit and general
features of them all are the same, each has its peculiar-
ities.   Without attempting any detail of these, I will
quote one or two passages from his account of "the hells
of those who have passed their lives in adulteries and
lasciviousness," and leave the reader to form his own
judgment.

"Those who find their chief delight in the spoils of
virginity, having no regard to marriage or issue, and
who, after compassing their lustful ends, conceive an
aversion for their victims, and then leave them to prostitution, suffer the most grievous punishment in the other
world.   For their life is contrary to all order, natural,
spiritual, and celestial.   Not only is it contrary to conjugial love, which in heaven is accounted most holy, but
also to innocence, which they wound and destroy by se-
ducing innocent beings into a course of prostitution, who
might have been initiated into conjugial love; for the
first delights of love, as is well known, introduce virgins
to chaste conjugial love, and conjoin the minds of mar-
ried partners.   And since the sanctity of heaven is

founded on conjugial love, and on innocence, the destroyers of such love must needs be murderers interiorly."

And after giving some account of the terrible punishment which this class of persons have to suffer in the other world, he continues:

"This punishment returns many times for a hundred and a thousand years, until they become affected with horror at these lusts. I have been informed that the offspring of such parents are worse than other children on account of their constitution, derived hereditarily from the father, partaking of his nature. Therefore children are seldom born from such connections; or if they are, they do not remain long in this world."—A. C. 828.

And what does he say of the innocent victims of these wicked persons, some of whom he met in the other world?

"There are young girls who have been enticed to prostitution, and persuaded that there was no evil in it, who in other respects were well disposed. These, not having yet attained to an age capable of knowing and judging correctly of the nature of this kind of life, have a certain instructor set over them in the other world, who is very severe, and chastises them whenever they give their thoughts to such wantonness, and of whom they are much afraid. In this way they become vastated." That is, they are carried through a certain reformatory course of discipline; and "when the time of vastation is over, they are taken up into heaven; and being novitiates,

13 *

they are instructed in the truths of faith by the angels among whom they are received."—A. C. 1106, '13.

But very different is it with another class of females whom he met in the spiritual world, and who were, when on earth, persons of most captivating manners, but deceitful, ambitious and destitute of conscience.

"There are some of the female sex who have lived in the indulgence of their inclinations, regarding only themselves and the world, and making the sum total of life and its delights to consist in external decorum, in consequence of which they have been particularly esteemed in polished society. They have thus, by practice, acquired the power of insinuating themselves into the good graces of others by specious pretences and a fair exterior, for the purpose of gaining an ascendency over them. Hence their life has been one of simulation and deceit. They used to frequent churches like other people, but for no other purpose than to appear upright and pious; being, moreover, destitute of conscience, and extremely prone to wickedness and adulteries when able to conceal them. Such persons in the other world think as they did here, not knowing what conscience is, and making a mock of those who speak of it. They enter into the affections of others by a pretended honesty, piety, compassion, and innocence, which with them are a means of deceiving; and whenever external restraints are removed, they plunge into the most wicked and obscene practices. These are they who in the other world become enchantresses or sorceresses, some of whom are denominated sirens, who become expert in arts unknown on earth."

Some of these arts are described. "They can assume the likeness of others" at will. By cunning artifice "they can inspire every one with an affection for them." "They have the power of representing to the view of spirits a bright flame encompassing the head, and this— which is an angelic token—to several at the same moment. They can feign innocence by various methods, even by representing infants whom they kiss; they also excite others whom they hate to murder them. . . . Their nature is so persuasive that no one suspects them; and hence their ideas are not communicated like those of other spirits; for they have eyes resembling those ascribed to serpents, seeing every way at once, and having their thoughts present everywhere.

"These sorceresses or sirens are punished grievously, some in Gehenna, others in a kind of court among serpents; others by being, as it were, torn asunder and subjected to various collisions attended with intensest pain and torture."—Ibid. 831.

And this, too, for their own good. For there is nothing of vindictiveness in the punishments of hell. They are all repressive, corrective and reformatory in their design and tendency.

But will the hells remain forever as they were when Swedenborg saw them? Is there to be no change—no

improvement—in their condition? If so, of what nature?—and how is the improvement to be effected? The
answer to these questions has been already anticipated in
a measure; but I will endeavor to make it clearer and
more definite.

"The Lord is good to all, and his tender mercies are
over all his works." He, therefore, has regard for, and
continually endeavors to promote the best good even of
the devils. He governs the hells as well as the heavens;
and his love and wisdom are as conspicuous and as
active in the one realm as in the other. But the devils
cannot be governed in the same way, or by the same
methods, as the angels. The latter, because they love
the Lord above all things, and their neighbor even better
than themselves, can be led and governed by love—by
the love of what is just and true and good. But the
former, since they have no love of the Lord or their
neighbor, but love themselves supremely, can be governed only by fear. Self-love is perpetually encroaching
upon the rights of others; perpetually grasping at un-
limited power; perpetually seeking, not to serve and
bless others, but to subjugate them to its own control.
It is, therefore, from its very nature, forever threatening
the peace and welfare of the moral universe. And the
only way this love can be restrained in its insane endeavors, is through fear—the fear of punishment.

The only way, therefore, that the Lord can reach the
hells, and exert upon them a controlling influence, is

through the medium of fear. It is in this way that He comes to, and manifests his love for, the devils. He does not hate them. He does not turn his face away from them. He does not take delight in tormenting them, as Christians have hitherto believed and taught;—far from it. On the contrary his love for them is like that of a kind and benignant father for his disobedient children, only infinitely more tender. It is not less strong for them, than it is for men on earth, or even for the angels in heaven;—no, nor less active in its efforts to promote their highest welfare. But because they have quenched his holy Spirit in their hearts—because they have refused to listen to his loving voice, which evermore seeks to lead men freely in the path to heaven, therefore they must be governed like wayward and rebellious children. They cannot be governed as the angels are—by love; they can only be governed by fear. Therefore the Lord permits them to be punished from time to time, with more or less severity according to the stubbornness of their dispositions or the measure of their perversity. And this, too, for their own good; precisely as a wise and loving father will chastise his disobedient children, not because he delights in causing them pain, but because he wishes, *for their good*, to subdue their rebellious dispositions, and prevent them from injuring themselves and others through the unrestrained indulgence of their wrong inclinations.

It is precisely in this way that the Lord deals with the

evil spirits in hell—*his* disobedient and rebellious children. He permits them to suffer punishment from time
to time, but never without an end of use ;—never, but
for their own or others' good. As Swedenborg says:
"The Lord turns all punishment and torment [in the
other life] to some good use. It would be impossible
that there should be any such thing as punishment, unless *use* were the end aimed at by the Lord ; for the
Lord's kingdom is a kingdom of ends and uses." (*Arcana Cœlestia* 696.)

And this is the use intended by punishment in the
hells, and the use which it actually accomplishes : It
excites fear and dread by the pain it produces ; and thus
the devils are constrained, through fear of punishment,
to moderate their insanities, and restrain in some measure their evil inclinations. And although the lust of
doing evil forever remains, yet the condition of the
devils is rendered vastly more tolerable when they have
been reduced to a state in which they *dare* not do the
evil to which they are inclined ; and are kept in this
state through fear of punishment.

Under a government of fear and force, therefore—the
only kind of government suited to the states of the infernals—and through the instrumentality of punishments
administered by divine permission, a change in the condition of the hells is perpetually going on, though not
such an internal reformation as will result in obliterating

their existence, or in finally converting the devils into angels. Swedenborg says:

"All the inhabitants of hell are governed by fears; some, by fears implanted in the world, which still retain their influence; but because these fears are not sufficient, and likewise lose their force by degrees, they are governed by fear of punishment; and this fear is the principal means of deterring them from doing evil. The punishments in hell are various, more mild or more severe according to the nature of the evils to be restrained. For the most part the more malignant who excel in cunning and artifice, and are able to keep the rest in a state of submission and slavery by punishments and the terror thereby inspired, are set over the others; but these governors dare not go beyond the limits prescribed to them. It is to be observed that the fear of punishment is the only means of restraining the violence and fury of the hells: there is no other."—*Heaven and Hell* 543.

"They who have not in the world acknowledged the Lord, and that all good and truth are from Him and nothing from man, cannot resist evils as of themselves after death; for they are in evils and in the delight thereof grounded in love; and to resist the delight of their love, is to resist themselves, their own nature and their own life. On one occasion the experiment was made whether they were able to resist evils while the punishments of hell were announced to them, yea, while

they were seen and likewise felt; but it was in vain, for
they hardened their minds, saying, let come what will,
provided only that we are in the delight and joy of our
hearts while we are here. We shall not suffer more evil
than many others. But after a stated time they are cast
into hell, where they are compelled by punishments not
to do evil; but punishments do not take away the
will, the purpose, and consequent thought of evil;
they only prevent the evil act."—*Apocalypse Explained*
n. 1165.

"While man lives in the world, he is kept continually
in a state capable of being reformed, provided he desists
from evil from a free principle. But his life follows him
after death, and he remains in the state which he had
procured to himself by the whole course of his life in the
world. Then he who was in evil, is no longer capable
of being reformed; and lest he should have communication with any society of heaven, all truth and good are
taken away from him, in consequence of which he remains in the evil and false, which principles increase according to the faculty of receiving them which he has
acquired in the world; but he is not permitted to pass
beyond the acquired bounds. . . . His state then is such
that he cannot any longer be amended as to his interiors,
but only as to his exteriors; and this by fear of punishments, which, being often repeated, compel the spirit at
last to abstain from evil, which he does, not in freedom
but through compulsion, the lust of doing evil still re-

maining; this lust is held in check by fears, as was said, which fears are the external and compulsory means of amendment. Such is the state of the evil in the other life."—*Arcana Cœlestia* 6977.

"Every evil spirit in the other life brings punishment and torment on himself, by casting himself into the midst of the diabolical crew who act as the executioners. The Lord never sends any one into hell, but desires to bring all *out* of hell; still less does He inflict torment. But as the evil spirit rushes into it himself, the Lord turns all punishment and torment to some good account. There would be no such thing as punishment if *use* were not the end aimed at by the Lord; for his kingdom is a kingdom of ends and uses; but the uses which infernal spirits are able to perform are most ignoble; yet when they are engaged in the performance of these uses, they are not in a state of so great misery [as at other times]."
—Ibid. 696.

"Man in the other life enters into new states and undergoes changes. They who are being elevated into heaven, and afterwards when they have been elevated, advance forever towards perfection. But they who are being cast into hell, and afterwards when they have been cast in, endure sufferings more and more grievous, which are continued until they *dare* not do evil to any one. And afterwards they remain in hell to eternity. They cannot be drawn out, because they cannot be gifted with the ability to do good to any one, only *not to do evil* from

14

fear of punishment, the lust of doing it always remaining.''
—Ibid. 7541.

Such, then, is the nature of the change that is going on
in the hells, and such the means by which it is accomplished.   And even in the punishments which are there
inflicted, we have a manifestation of the Divine benevolence.   For the purpose of these is, the amelioration of
the condition of the devils ;—an end altogether worthy
of infinite Love, but one which infinite Wisdom sees
could not be attained without the instrumentality of punishment.   To withhold the exercise of this instrumentality, therefore, would not be an act of benevolence, and
hence not agreeable to infinite Love ; for this Love forever regards the end to be accomplished, and wisely permits temporary suffering as a means toward the attain-
ment of that end.

Through the instrumentality of punishments, therefore,
severe and oft-repeated, the hells are undergoing an improvement not unlike that which goes on in a well governed penitentiary here on earth.   They are being reformed outwardly, but not inwardly ;—not as to their
spirit or ruling purpose, for no internal reformation is
ever effected by punishment or the fear of it.   All that
punishment can ever do, is to intimidate and restrain,
and so prevent the actual commission of evil deeds, the
disposition to commit them still remaining.

By means of a strong police and severe punishments, a
community of thieves and murderers may be restrained,

and kept in some degree of external order; but theft and murder (or the spirit that prompts them) still remain in their hearts; and will break forth into outward act as soon as the police are out of the way, or there is no longer any fear of punishment. You cannot *drive* love—pure, unselfish love—into human hearts with bullets or bludgeons, by infantry or artillery, by cavalry or police.

Our state prisons furnish a good illustration of the hells as described by Swedenborg; and the external improvement which has been going on in many of these for the last thirty years, through a wise administration and a firm government, will give us some idea of the nature and extent of the improvement that is going on in the hells. And while this is not such as will result in finally changing their essential character or ruling love, let us hope that it may, however, be carried so far as to render the condition of the devils quite tolerable if not happy. Let us hope that, ultimately, they may be reduced to such a state of external order, that life—even the low and selfish kind of life which they have chosen and made their own—will be esteemed by them a blessing and not a curse.

In a community here on earth, where a great majority of the people have a conscience and are actuated by principle, the sphere of law and order, of justice and right, is usually so strong that there is rarely any outbreak of the hells through the minority. These latter are kept in subjection and order by purely selfish and prudential considerations—from an enlightened regard to their own temporal interests, or through fear of disgrace, punishment, or worldly loss of some sort. So from like considerations, and under the rigid discipline to which the devils are subjected and which I have here hastily outlined, the universal hell may ultimately be brought into such complete subjection to the angelic heaven, (whose numbers and influence, it is believed, are continually increasing), that the violent commotions and outbreaks which are now so frequent, will entirely cease. When this takes place, we can easily see that, although the hells will still remain unchanged as to their essential nature, they will be like the tamed tiger—submissive, and therefore harmless. We can see, too, that, by their subjection to the heaven of angels, or to the emanating and controlling sphere of law and order, their own peace and comfort will be increased, and the welfare of the moral universe promoted to an extent beyond the power of imagination to conceive.

Such is a brief outline of the New Doctrine of Hell; —a doctrine which builds itself impregnably upon the constitution and laws of the human soul, which accords with the teaching of sound philosophy, with the dictates of reason, with the facts of history, with the record of human experience, and with the teachings of Scripture rationally and spiritually interpreted.

How different this doctrine is from the one taught in

the literal sense of the Word, and generally accepted among Christians a hundred years ago! It presents us not with an angry and vindictive God delighting in the sufferings of his disobedient children, but with a tender and loving Father pitying their infirmities, and pursuing them with outstretched arms of mercy through all their wanderings, and even into the lowest depths of degradation and sin. And if, in the exercise of the freedom vouchsafed to every human being, they choose to unfold only the lower or sensuous part of their nature—*choose* to make their bed in hell, behold the loving Father is there, restraining, correcting, controlling and governing them in the manner best suited to their condition and needs; chastising them for their own good, and granting them the enjoyment of such delights as belong to the life which they have developed within them and made their own; mercifully closing their minds against the light of heaven, that they may not see where and what they really are; providing for each and all a home in the society of congenial spirits—a home which their nature impels them to seek, and to which they go as freely and as willingly as the inebriate goes to the gin-shop or the leopard to his lair.

And the practical tendency of this doctrine, like that of every other that is true, is most salutary. While it proclaims the infinite love and mercy of God, and his ceaseless desire and effort to save all, it at the same time shows us that salvation is a work which not even almighty

14 *   L

Love itself can accomplish *without our willing co-operation;* that the heavenly life cannot be *forced* upon us nor *into* us by almighty power, but can only be wrought out by our own volition—or built up through struggle and conflict and self-denial and obedience to the laws of that life,—the Lord meanwhile "working in us to will and to do of his good pleasure"; and that unless we *begin* to live the life of heaven here on earth—*begin* to deny self, take up the cross and follow the Master—we shall have no desire to engage in this work in the realm beyond the grave. The heaven of our minds will then be closed in tender compassion for us; and the peace and joy and unutterable bliss of heaven will, therefore, never be ours.

So tremendous are the moral sanctions with which this new doctrine is invested! So benign and quicken· ing is it in its practical tendency!

XI.

THE DEVIL AND SATAN.

NO treatise upon the subject that has thus far engaged our attention, would be satisfactory to an inquiring mind, which did not embrace an explanation of the terms *Devil* and *Satan.* These words occur very often in the New Testament, and in the closest possible connection with the term *Hell.* What is Swedenborg's explanation of them? Or what is the doctrine revealed through him concerning the Devil and Satan?

We know what doctrine had been generally taught and accepted by Christians up to the time he wrote. It was that of a personal Devil—an individual of unparalleled malignity, the implacable enemy of both God and man, and endued with little less than omnipotent power. And this idea agrees with the *literal* teaching of the Bible. It also appears from the literal sense of some passages (and this, too, has been the accepted doctrine among Christians) as if this almost omnipotent evil spirit, was once an inhabitant of the highest heaven—foremost among the heavenly host in wisdom and all angelic graces;—one

" ——who, in the happy realms of light,
Clothed with transcendent brightness, did outshine
Myriads though bright;"——

but who, on account of his impious attempt to overthrow
the divine government and establish himself on the
throne of the universe, was cast down from heaven, and
became thereby the prince of the bottomless pit, the
commander in chief of all the hosts of hell. (See Is.
xii. 14; Jude 6th v.; Rev. ix. 11.)

Such was the generally accepted doctrine of the Devil
a hundred years ago. And it is believed by many at the
present day. A high authority where definitions are in
question (Noah Webster), defines *Satan* to be "the grand
adversary of man; the devil, or prince of darkness; the
chief of the fallen angels; the arch-fiend." And in an
abridgement of his great work, we find *Devil* defined
thus:—"In the *Christian theology*—a fallen angel ex-
pelled from heaven for rebellion against God; the chief
of the fallen angels."

From these definitions we learn that the notion which
Christians have generally attached to these words, has
been precisely that expressed by Milton in his great epic,
where he introduces Satan as one

" ——cast out from heaven, with all his host
Of rebel angels; by whose aid aspiring
To set himself in glory above his peers,
He trusted to have equaled the Most High
If He opposed; and with ambitious aim

Against the throne and monarchy of God,
Raised impious war in heaven, and battle proud,
With vain attempt. Him the almighty Power
Hurled headlong flaming from the ethereal sky,
With hideous ruin and combustion, down
To bottomless perdition; there to dwell
In adamantine chains and penal fire,
Who durst defy the Omnipotent to arms."

But there are not a few at the present day, both within and outside of all the churches—and their number is steadily increasing—who do not believe a word of this old and once popular doctrine of the Devil. They reject that whole story about the war in heaven, and the overthrow and expulsion of the rebel hosts, as fabulous. And if any one is curious to know the origin of this notion about the "fallen angels," let him read attentively the critical remarks of Dr. Moses Stuart on the Apochryphal book of Enoch, from which it is evident that the apostle Jude quoted. The conclusion of this learned writer is briefly stated thus: "Probable I must deem it to be, that Jude has quoted the book of Enoch; because he seems, in what he says of the angels who kept not their first estate, but left their habitation and are reserved in chains of darkness, to allude to the account of apostate angels as given in the book of Enoch." (*Stuart on the Apocalypse*, Vol. I., p. 51–73.)

The old doctrine on this subject, then, is clearly one that belongs to a superstitious and unenlightened age.

It bears about it the air of fable. Our reason and the enlightened sentiment of the present day repudiate it utterly.

Let us turn, now, to the new doctrine revealed through Swedenborg; and see if that be as unreasonable or improbable as the old. What, according to this new revelation, *is* the Devil and Satan of Scripture?

Consider that evil spirits are not all in the same kind or degree of evil. They are not all alike, any more than men on earth or angels in heaven. There are innumerable varieties of evil in hell, as there are of good in heaven. And those who are in similar kinds and degrees of evil, prefer to be together. They are therefore drawn by the law of spiritual affinity into the same society. Every devil is carried to that particular society whose general character most nearly resembles his own. There he finds himself at home. He is drawn to it by an irresistible attraction—for in the other world each one goes where his ruling love leads him. Spirits can no more resist or cut themselves loose from the law of spiritual attraction, than our earth can resist or cut itself loose from the law of material attraction.

By virtue of this law, and of the endless variety of goods and evils in the other world, both in kind and in degree, there are in heaven and in hell a countless number of societies, each one of which is in some specific kind and degree of good or evil. All the societies in heaven, viewed collectively, constitute one gigantic Man or Angel; and are often called by Swedenborg *Maximus Homo*—the Grand Man. The meaning of this is, that the connection, interdependence, and mutual relation of the innumerable societies composing the whole angelic heaven, and the uses which they severally perform, correspond to the harmonious relation existing between the different organs of the human body, and their respective functions.

And since the mutual relation and dependence of all the angelic societies is such that the whole heaven appears before the Lord as one symmetrical and colossal Man or Angel, so the infernal societies are so related and united that all hell appears as one gigantic and deformed Monster or Devil. The difference in their appearance corresponds exactly to the difference in their character. And this is as the difference between a single angel and devil, one of whom is a form of all that is pure and good, and therefore indescribably beautiful; the other a form of all that is evil and loathsome, and therefore hideous.

This, according to Swedenborg, is what we are to understand by the *Devil* and *Satan* so often mentioned in Scripture. Each of these is a collective term when used in its widest sense, and denotes all the infernal societies viewed as a single individual. There is an organic connection among infernal spirits. One life pervades them all, and that is the life of self-love and the lusts therein originating,—just as one kind of blood, pure or impure, courses through all parts of the human body even to its remotest extremities. And as the whole body conspires in producing the slightest motion of any limb—a foot, an arm, a hand or a finger—so all hell conspires in the perpetration of every wicked deed—in every evil purpose, word, or work.

We see, then, that, according to the New doctrine, no single individual as chief of the fallen angels, is meant by these Scripture terms, but all evil spirits in the complex,—or some one of the infernal societies with whose every act and purpose the whole conspires. *Devil* is the term employed when hell is spoken of with more especial reference to the evil loves that reign there; and *Satan*, when it is spoken of with more especial reference to its false persuasions.

And because all hell is in a state of opposition to what is good and true, and perpetually conspires to destroy man spiritually, by the sphere of evil and falsity which continually issues from it as a poisonous exhalation, therefore we read that the Devil "was a murderer from the beginning, and abode not in the truth because there is no truth in him. When he speaketh a lie, he speaketh of his own [i. e., according to his own nature]; for he is a liar and the father of it." Nothing but falsity is in agreement with evil. Therefore nothing but lies can come forth from the hearts of those who are essentially evil—supremely selfish—when they speak from their own nature.

So reasonable is the view here presented, and so much more satisfactory than the Old doctrine, that we are not surprised to find it beginning to be accepted by some of the acutest minds and profoundest thinkers even among those commonly reputed orthodox. To cite here, by way of illustration, a single passage from that most fascinating work, *Nature and the Supernatural,* from the pen of Dr. Horace Bushnell, unquestionably one of the ablest theologians in America. Speaking of the doctrine of the Manichees or disciples of Zoroaster, this writer says :

"If their good principle, called God by us, is taken as a being, and their bad principle as only a condition privative ; one as a positive and real cause, the other as a bad possibility that environs God from eternity, waiting to become a fact and certain to become a fact whenever the opportunity is given, it is even so. And then it follows that the moment God creates a realm of powers, the bad possibility as certainly becomes a bad actuality, a Satan, or Devil, *in esse;* not a bad omnipresence over against God, and his equal—that is a monstrous and horrible conception—but an outbreaking evil or empire of evil in created spirits, according to their order. For Satan, or the Devil, taken in the singular, is not the name of any particular person, neither is it a personation merely of temptation, or impersonal evil, as many insist ; for there is really no such thing as impersonal evil in the sense of moral evil ; but the name is a name that

15

generalizes bad persons or spirits, with their bad thoughts or characters, many in one. That there is any single one of them who, by distinction or pre-eminence, is called Satan, or Devil, is wholly improbable. The name is one taken up by the imagination, to designate or embody, in a conception the mind can most easily wield, the all or total of bad minds or powers."—pp. 134, '5.

I do not know whether this learned writer derived the view here expressed from Swedenborg, or whether he reached it by a kind of spiritual intuition. In either case the testimony of such a mind is equally valuable. The doctrine, we see, is identically the same as that revealed through Swedenborg.

Pursuing our inquiry,—we find that the word *Angel* is used in Scripture in a manner similar to the word *Devil*, as explained by Swedenborg. Sometimes it is used to denote a single individual, sometimes a single angelic society, and sometimes the whole angelic heaven which is an angel in the largest form. Thus the seer of Patmos speaks of the angels of the churches of Ephesus, Smyrna, Thyatira, etc., by which are meant the angelic societies connected with and presiding over these churches. We read also in Psalms: "The angel of the Lord encampeth round about them that fear Him, and delivereth them." Here "the angel of the Lord" means the whole angelic heaven.

But heaven is the same in each and all of its parts, as it is in the whole. Therefore the word *angel*, which is sometimes used in Scripture to denote the whole angelic heaven, or some society thereof, is also used in the plural (*angels*) to denote two or more individuals; for every angel is a heaven in the smallest form.

Similar remarks may be made with reference to the use of the word *devil.* It is used in the singular as a collective term to denote all hell in the complex; and again we find the same word often used in the plural (*devils*), denoting individual evil spirits, or the constituent parts of hell, which are similar in character to the whole.

We use the term *man* in precisely the same way. We sometimes apply it to a single individual, and sometimes to the race. It is often used in this latter sense in the Bible, as a collective term. As where it is said: "God made man in his own image." "Man shall not live by bread alone, but by every word that proceedeth out of the mouth of God shall man live." Again we use this word in the plural (*men*), when speaking of a number of individuals, or of mankind in general.

And what is more common than to hear a country, a kingdom, or state, or other community of persons spoken of as a single individual. Every one speaks of England, France, Germany, the United States, etc., or the people of these countries viewed collectively, as one person, with the same familiarity and the same confidence of being understood, as he would speak of Mr. Smith or Mr. Jones, his next door neighbor.

Now if *Man* is often used as a collective term to denote
the entire human race, and *Angel* in like manner to denote the whole angelic heaven, why should not *Devil*
be used in the same way to denote all evil spirits in the
complex? or, as Dr. Bushnell expresses it, "the total
of bad minds"? These are all animated by one and
the same bad spirit; they all breathe hatred, cruelty,
revenge and murder; they are all joined in an alliance
of evil; they all conspire to work deeds of darkness;
and viewed collectively, what are they but one inhuman
Monster or Devil?

And this view has the clear testimony of Scripture as
well as of reason in its support. For we read of one
"that was possessed with the devil," who was "always,
night and day, in the mountains and in the tombs,
crying and cutting himself with stones." This poor,
devil-possessed creature met Jesus as He came out of the
ship; and as soon as he saw Him "he ran and worshiped
Him, and cried with a loud voice, and said, What have
I to do with thee, Jesus, thou Son of the most high
God?" And Jesus, commanding the unclean spirit to
come out of the man, "asked him, What is thy name?
And he answered, saying, My name is Legion; for we
are many."—Mark v. 9. And immediately after, this
same unclean spirit, called in verses 15 and 16 "the
devil," is spoken of in the plural as "the unclean spirits,"
and "*all* the devils."

There are a number of other names by which the Devil

is called in Scripture, each of which expresses something of the essential nature of hell; such as, Angel of the bottomless pit, Prince of this world, Prince of darkness, Destroyer, Beelzebub, Belial, Adversary, Accuser, Deceiver, Liar, Murderer, Tormentor, Serpent, Lucifer, Leviathan and Dragon. Such are the significant names which we find in the Bible sometimes applied to the collective body of evil spirits in the other world, who, viewed as one individual, are more frequently called the Devil and Satan. And how completely do such names justify the following language of Swedenborg:

"As heaven, from the Lord, by mutual love, constitutes as it were one Man or one soul, and thus regards one end which is the preservation and salvation of all to eternity; so on the other hand hell, from proprium, by self-love and the love of the world, that is, by hatred, constitutes one Devil or one mind, and thus regards one end, which is the destruction and damnation of all to eternity. That such is the tendency of each has been granted me to perceive many thousands of times." (*Arcana Cœlestia* 694.)

We thus see that the New doctrine on this, as on other subjects, is quite different from the Old. The Devil, according to Swedenborg's disclosures, is not the personal one described by Milton, and hitherto believed in by Christians generally. Nor is he a fabulous or imaginary being, but one whose existence and reality the philosphic inquirer readily admits. Nay, he is one

15 *

whose existence we are *compelled* to admit, the moment
we admit that each one takes his own character with him
into the other world, and that those of similar character
are there drawn together, and held together and act together as one.

And something—nay, much, I think—is gained, when
the Devil, whom intelligent people were fast coming to
look upon as a fabulous sort of being, is so presented
that all doubt about his existence and reality as well as
his nature, is banished.   It places the Scripture in a different light, and inspires fresh confidence in its divinity.

And seeing what the essential nature of the Devil is,
we may see what it is to be influenced and led by him—
and what to be led by the Lord.   When we earnestly strive
to know and do the right—when we look to the Lord
and seek to regulate our lives according to his revealed
will, then we suffer ourselves to be led and governed by
Him.

But when we seek only to do our own wills—when we
heed the promptings of self-love more than the still small
voice of truth and duty, then we breathe the atmosphere
of hell ; our spirits act in conjunction with the infernals ;
we are led and governed by the Devil.

And when we consider what legions there are who constitute the Devil, and who are banded together in a con-
spiracy against all that is good and true and holy in
human hearts and human society, how clear and imper-
ative becomes the need of an almighty Arm to save us !

and how earnestly should we seek the Divine protecting sphere! How anxious should we be to know the truth, and how careful to govern our lives according to its requirements—ever acknowledging the Lord's own immediate presence and power in the truths we learn and do! This is the only way we can secure for ourselves the protection of that Arm which alone can shield us against the power of hell.

How imminent is our spiritual danger, how watchful we ought to be over our hearts and lives, how much we need the Divine protection, and how that protection is best ensured, will appear from the following extract from Swedenborg's *Heaven and Hell:*

"Every spirit is his own good or his own evil, because he is his own love. Therefore, as an angelic spirit thinks, wills, speaks, and acts from his own good, so does an infernal spirit from his own evil; and to think, will, speak, and act, from evil itself, is to do so from all the things which are included in the evil. It was otherwise when he lived in the body. The evil of the man's spirit was then restrained by the bonds, in which every one is held by the law, by his love of gain and honor, and through fear of losing them; on which account the evil of his spirit could not then break out, and manifest itself in its own intrinsic nature. Besides, the evil of the man's spirit then lay wrapped up and veiled in external probity, sincerity, justice, and the affection of truth and good, of which such a man has made an oral profession, and has assumed an appearance for the sake of the world. Under these outward semblances, the evil lay so covered up and concealed, that he was scarcely aware himself that his spirit contained so great wickedness and subtlety, or that in himself he was such a devil as he becomes after death, when his spirit comes into itself, and into its own nature. Such wickedness then manifests itself as exceeds all belief. There are thousands of evils which burst forth from evil itself, among which, also, are such as cannot be expressed in the words of any language. I have been permitted to learn and comprehend their nature by much experience ; for it has been granted me by the Lord to be in the spiritual world as to my spirit, and at the same time in the natural world as to my body. This I can testify, that their wickedness is so great, that it is hardly possible to describe a thousandth part of it; and furthermore, that unless the Lord protected man, it would be impossible for him ever to be rescued from hell; for there are with every man both spirits from hell and angels from heaven; and the Lord cannot protect a man, unless he acknowledge the Divine, and live the life of faith and charity; for otherwise, he averts himself from the Lord, and turns toward infernal spirits, and thus becomes imbued as to his spirit with similar wickedness."—577.

XII.

PRACTICAL BEARINGS OF THE QUESTION.

BESIDES this outer world of matter, there is another realm of being;—a world of spirits, both good and evil;—a heaven of angels and a hell of devils. Nor is this realm remote from the world in which we are now living and acting, but intimately present with it, inter-penetrating every part of it, as the soul of man pervades and animates every part of his body.

In the midst of this viewless host our own souls live and breathe and act. With one or another class of spirits we internally hold close companionship; and are powerfully influenced by them for good or for evil. Neither heaven nor hell are far-away, but present and potential realities—none the less so because their deni-zens are invisible to the natural eye. And the moment this fact is recognized, the important practical bearings of the subject discussed in these pages, becomes apparent. For if hell be a present reality, or if it can come near to men and exert upon them a potent influence, it is import-ant that we understand its nature.

And all who accept the Sacred Scripture as a revelation from God, must recognize this fact. For on almost every page of the Bible, the existence of a realm above nature—of a world peopled by spirits, good and evil—is clearly implied if not distinctly asserted. Angels and devils are spoken of as often, and with as much familiarity, as are any other objects whose reality no one ever dreamed of questioning. Their existence is everywhere assumed. There is never an attempt to prove it, any more than there is to prove the existence of the sun, moon or stars.

Angels are spoken of as often seen by persons in the flesh; as conversing with and sustaining an intimate relation to them; as feeling a lively interest in humanity, and exerting an influence upon the condition of mortals. They were seen, for example, by Jacob, Gideon, Manoah, Zacharias, the shepherds of Bethlehem, and the women "who were early at the sepulchre." Myriads of them were beheld, and their voices heard, by John when he was in the spirit. And as evidence of their interest in and their sympathy with people here on earth, we are told in the gospel of Luke that "there is joy in the presence of the angels of God over one sinner that repenteth."

Equally explicit, too, is the Scripture in its teaching respecting evil spirits or devils, and their malign influence upon the inhabitants of this world. When our Saviour was on earth, multitudes were possessed by them; and we are told that "He cast out the devils with his word." He also gave his disciples "power over unclean spirits to cast them out." And when He sent them forth to preach the gospel of the Kingdom, He gave them a commission to "heal the sick, cleanse the lepers, raise the dead, and *cast out devils.*" When the evil spirits saw Him, they (or the persons possessed by them) cried out for fear, fell down before Him, or quickly fled away as from one whose sphere was insufferably painful. And "with authority," it is said, "He commandeth the unclean spirits, and they obey Him." And on one occasion when He was met by a poor demoniac who had his dwelling among the tombs, "He said unto him, Come out of the man, thou unclean spirit." And when he was asked "What is thy name?" he answered "My name is Legion; for we are many."

Then look at the character of the Devil as portrayed in the Bible;—and this term, as shown in the previous chapter, is applied to the congregated hosts of hell, or all evil spirits viewed collectively. His character is clearly indicated by the several names applied to him. For he is called a liar, a destroyer, the accurser of the brethren, the adversary, the deceiver, a murderer, the old serpent, the tempter, the wicked one, the spirit that worketh in the children of disobedience. He is represented, moreover, as the enemy of God and the human race; as opposed to the establishment of the Redeemer's kingdom, or to the reign of justice, liberty and love in human hearts; as earnestly bent on man's destruction; as the inspirer of all wicked thoughts, and malign pur-

poses; as putting it into the heart of Judas Iscariot to
betray the blessed Saviour; as corrupting and misleading
men by craft and subtlety; as "going about like a roar-
ing lion, seeking whom he may devour."

The Scripture testimony on this subject is abundant
and conclusive. We see not how it could be more explicit. If the existence of an innumerable company of
angels and devils, their close proximity to man, and their
intense desire and earnest effort, the one class to do him
good and the other to do him harm, be not plainly taught
in the Bible, then it would be difficult, I think, to say
what *is* plainly taught there.

And yet the explicit teaching of Scripture on this momentous theme, has come to be quite overlooked or
ignored by many Christians; and so explained by others
as to cast doubt on the very existence of spirits, good or
evil. These facts go to show how important it was that
some one should be intromitted into the spiritual world
in the manner that Swedenborg was (or, if you please,
claimed to be), that he might thereby be enabled to make
a truthful revelation concerning that world.

That the practical bearings of the question discussed
in these pages, may be more distinctly seen, I will give
a brief outline of the spiritual world, even at the risk of
treading upon some ground that has already been trav-
eled over.

I observe, then, that the spiritual world is one of substantial realities—more real, indeed, than the one in

which we are now living. It is not remote from this world as to space, but is intimately present with it as the soul is with the body. It is peopled by a countless multitude of beings, all of whom are in the human form and were once inhabitants of the natural world. These are organized in general into two grand divisions,—a heaven of angels and a hell of devils. The angels are distributed into innumerable societies, corresponding, in their mutual relations and in the functions they respectively perform, to the different members and organs of the human body; so that together they constitute one Grand Man or Angel. And to the Lord they actually appear as one, and constitute his heavenly kingdom. These are spoken of in the Bible as "the angel of the Lord" and "the host of heaven."

And the angels are all good and wise, although there is a wide diversity of character among them. Some are in a high and others in a comparatively low degree of wisdom; some in one kind of good, others in another. But love to the Lord and the neighbor is the chief inspiration—yea, the very life-blood of all their hearts. They are all, to some extent, images and likenesses of the Lord. They have been with Him and learned of Him;—learned to be meek and lowly in heart, forgetful of themselves and thoughtful only of the good of others;—learned to do justly, to love mercy, and to walk humbly with their God. These constitute that bright angelic throng, of whom it is said that they

16

"came out of great tribulation, and have washed their robes and made them white in the blood of the Lamb." They are all of them children of the Heavenly Father, having their hearts stamped indelibly with the impress of his spirit—which is what is meant by their having "his name written in their foreheads." Their love is like God's, pure and unselfish. They love each other even better than themselves, and find their chief delight in doing good and communicating happiness to others. Having in their hearts the very spirit of the Lord, they love only what He loves, and delight to do only those things that He delights to have them do. Their ruling desire and purpose are the same as his; their ends and aims the same. For they desire above all else to impart unto others the delights of heavenly life. They desire to dissipate the spiritual darkness, to heal the spiritual sickness, to restore the spiritual health and renew the spiritual strength of the world. Swedenborg's writings are full of the most beautiful and inspiring pictures of angelic life, from which people here on earth may learn lessons of the highest practical wisdom. Thus he says :

" The angelic life consists in the performance of uses, or in the goods of charity. For to the angels nothing is more delightful than to instruct spirits coming from the world ;—to serve mankind by inspiring them with what is good, and by restraining the evil spirits attendant on them from passing their proper bounds ;—to raise up the dead to eternal life, and afterwards, if their souls be of such a character as to render it possible, to introduce them into heaven. In the performance of these offices they experience an unspeakable delight. Thus they are images of the Lord, for they love their neighbor more than themselves; and where this feeling exists, there is heaven. Angelic happiness, therefore, is in use, from use, and according to use; or in other words, it is according to the goods of love and charity. . . .

"Some of the best educated [who were met with in the other world], declared heavenly joy to consist in a life separated from the good offices of charity and in merely praising and worshiping the Lord,—calling this an active life. They were told, however, that praising and worshiping the Lord, is not such an active life, but the effect of such life; for the Lord has no need of men's praises, but desires that they perform the good works of charity. According as they do these, they receive happiness from the Lord. Yet these most learned spirits could have no idea of delight, but of servitude, in these good works of charity; but the angels testified that such good offices are compatible with the most perfect freedom, and attended with inexpressible felicity."—*Arcana Cœlestia* 454, 456.

Again he says:

"Charity is nothing unless it manifests itself in works of charity. It exists only in exercise, or in the performance of uses. He who loves his neighbor as himself, never perceives the delight of charity except in its exercise, or in use; the life of charity, therefore, is a life of uses. Such is the life of the whole heaven; for the Lord's kingdom is a kingdom of uses, because a kingdom of mutual love. Therefore every pleasure derived from charity, has its delight from use; and the more exalted the use, so much the greater its delight. Hence the angels have happiness from the Lord according to the nature and quality of the uses they perform."— Ibid. 997.

Such is the nature of angelic life—the life which we are all made capable of attaining, and which the Lord is forever seeking to develop or build up within us. Such is the character of that heavenly kingdom whereof the Bible so often speaks—a kingdom of righteousness, joy and peace—a kingdom of pure and loving hearts—the very kingdom for which we pray when we breathe that inspired petition, "Thy kingdom come, thy will be done on earth as it is done in heaven."

And people are continually passing into that kingdom —passing from earth to heaven. What class of people? The Bible tells us. All those righteous ones who walked, while here below, in the law of the Lord;—those lowly ones who, through repentance and regeneration, have become as little children;—the meek, the merciful, the poor in spirit, the pure in heart, those who have practiced self-denial, and earnestly sought to do the will of the Father which is in the heavens.

We thus see what the kingdom of heaven is; and that all who enter that kingdom after death, must have heaven within themselves. That is, they must carry the loves and purposes that rule in heaven, and be able to find delight in such works as are delightful to the angels.

But there is another kingdom in the spiritual realm of which the Bible tells us—a hell of devils. These, too, are arranged, in like manner as the angels, into many different societies according to the kinds and degrees of evil in which they are. Nor is there anything arbitrary or compulsory in this arrangement. They come into it in perfect freedom. Each one goes into the society for which he has an affinity—into the one whose general character is nearest like his own. And these societies of evil spirits, like those in heaven, are all so united, that together they constitute one huge monster, called in Scripture "the Devil."

The character of these evil spirits is quite the opposite of that of the angels. They have no love of the Lord or the neighbor; and therefore know nothing of the heavenly delight resulting from the exercise of this love. The love of self is the supreme and ruling love of them all; and this is real hatred toward those who refuse to minister to its gratification.

And as self-love is the source of all other evil loves when it reigns supreme, therefore the devils are thoroughly immersed in evil. They are full of hatred, malice, craft and subtlety;—full of falsehood, tyranny,

16 *

cunning and cruelty. Their life is one of unmitigated
selfishness. It is their delight to do all manner of mischief;—to foment hatreds, strifes and divisions;—to stir
up envies, jealousies and revenges;—to intensify all the
worst passions of the human heart;—to blind, and mis-
lead, and if possible make slaves of, all who come within
the sphere of their influence.

Such, briefly, is the character of that legion of infernals in the spiritual world, who, taken collectively, are
called the Devil. What a contrast to the character
of those shining ones in the realms above!

Consider, now, that as to our spirits we are always
living in the spiritual world, even while clothed with
material flesh and blood; and are actually associated
with one or the other class of spirits above described.
We may flee the society of persons in the flesh; but we
can never be alone. We can never rid ourselves of the
society of spirits. Wherever we are, an invisible company attends us—in solitude no less than in society. We
do not see them, nor sensibly perceive their influence.
Yet their presence is none the less real on that account,
nor their influence less positive. We do not hear their
voices—certainly not with our outward ears; yet they
converse with us during all our waking hours. Through
the intricate and mysterious galleries of the soul they
whisper to us a blessed gospel of peace and good will—
thoughts of kindness, usefulness, justice, mercy, forbear-

ance, benevolence, and willing self-sacrifice for the good of others; or they suggest ways and means whereby our pride, vanity, ambition, lust of dominion, love of ease or pleasure, or selfish greed of gain, may most surely be gratified.

Yes: one or the other of these two classes of spirits,—according as we are more willing to listen to the soft pleadings of the angels, or to be beguiled by the glazing flattery of devils,—one or the other of these classes are our intimate associates, our bosom companions. Of one or the other we take counsel day by day, however unconscious we may be of the fact. To one or the other we listen from hour to hour. With one or the other we think and feel and act in the ordinary intercourse of our every-day life. There is no escape from this. The laws of our spiritual being, and the arrangements and constitution of the moral universe, render it a necessity. Our spirits breathe, and *must* breathe, the atmosphere of heaven or of hell. They may—oftentimes they do —breathe that of each by turns.

But the Lord vouchsafes to every one the liberty of choice. We are as free to choose our *invisible* as we are our visible associates. Nay, we *do* choose them, whether we think of it or not. We have actually chosen them, though it may not be for eternity; for we have the power to change our invisible as well as our visible companions. Indeed, the whole work of regeneration—every inward change we experience—involves a change in our spiritual associates, or the passing out of one spiritual society and the entering into another.

And now comes the momentous question: Is there any way of ascertaining the character of our invisible associates? Is there any test whereby we may know with certainty whether our spirits consort with angels or devils?—whether we inhale from day to day the balmy air of heaven, or the noxious and soul-disordering exhalations of hell?

Most undoubtedly. There is a universal law that governs all associations in the spiritual world—those in hell as well as those in heaven. It is the law of spiritual affinity which has been repeatedly spoken of in the foregoing pages. This law forever impels spirits to seek the companionship of those most like themselves. Under its operation, therefore, kindred spirits are drawn together and held together in the same society. Those in a similar kind and degree of good, or in a similar kind and degree of evil, have an affinity for each other. They love to be together. Their sphere is mutually agreeable. Therefore they gravitate toward each other by force of mutual attraction.

And it is this same law which determines the character of our invisible companions. Through its operation, spirits are attracted to us who are similar in character to ourselves. The prevailing tenor of our thoughts and affections—the nature of the love that rules in our hearts —the kind of motives from which we generally act—

the principles which govern us in our ordinary inter-course with men—these are the indices which reveal the character of our spiritual associates. If our prevailing desire and effort be to know and do the will of the Lord, then angels are our companions ; our spirits consort with the white-robed throng ; we breathe the atmosphere of heaven.

But if our ends be mean and selfish ; if we are heed-less of the Divine commands, or deaf to the still small voice of duty ; if our prevailing purpose be to do our own will· rather than the will of God ; then, our spiritual asso-ciates belong to the realms below ; we are in fellowship with devils ; we breathe the polluting air of hell.

We have but to look, therefore, at our governing prin-ciples of action—at our dominant feelings, dispositions and motives—at our chief end and aim in life, in order to learn the character of our invisible associates. Accord-ingly Swedenborg says :—

"All spirits are distinguished in the other life by this : They who intend evil to others, are infernal or diabolical spirits; but they who intend good to others, are good and angelic spirits. A man may know which class he is among, whether angelic or infernal spirits. If he intends evil to his neighbor, thinking nothing but evil concern-ing him, and actually doing him evil whenever it is in his power, and finding delight in doing it, then he is among the infernals, and also becomes an infernal him-self in the other life. But if he intends good to his neighbor, and thinks nothing but good respecting him, and actually does him good when it is in his power, then he is among angelic spirits, and also becomes an angel himself in the other life.

"This is the criterion. Let every one examine himself by it. It matters not that a person does not do evil when he either cannot or dare not, nor that he does good from some selfish consideration; such abstinence from the one and performance of the other, have their origin only in the man's externals; and these are removed in the other life, where he is such as his thoughts and intentions make him."—*Arcana Cælestia* n. 1680.

Again he says:

"A man's end is his very life; for that which belongs to his life, or what is the same thing, to his love, he regards as an end. When the good of the neighbor, the general good, the good of the church and of the Lord's kingdom is the end regarded, then the man as to his soul is in the Lord's kingdom; for His kingdom is none other than a kingdom of ends and uses having respect to the good of the human race. The angels themselves attendant on man, are in nothing else [or have regard to nothing else] but his ends. As far as a man's end is the same as that aimed at by the Lord's kingdom, so far the angels are delighted with him and unite themselves to him as to a brother; but in proportion as he is actuated by a selfish end, the angels recede, and evil spirits from hell draw near; for no other than a selfish end rules in hell.

"From these considerations it is evident how important it is for a man to examine and know the origin of his affections; and this can only be known from the end at which he aims."—Ibid. 3796.

In view of what has now been said, the practical bearings of this question are sufficiently obvious. When these great truths are recognized, that man is essentially a spiritual being; that, within our outer material vesture, is a spiritual and substantial body which continues to live after the material body perishes; that, as to our spirits we are now and always living in the spiritual world, in close companionship with an invisible company whose character is determined by our own governing motives and cherished purposes; that the character we form while here on earth will go with us into the other world, and continue essentially the same forever; that the spiritual associates we *now* choose and bind to us by an unfailing law, are the very ones whose companionship we shall prefer and seek in the life beyond the grave; that we are already *in* hell, however unconscious we may be of the fact, if our ends and aims be similar to those that rule in the realms below; and that our only hope of deliverance is in looking to the Lord in humble acknowledgment of our dependence on Him, and religiously obeying the laws of life that He has revealed;—when these truths, which are all involved in the New view of hell, are seen and acknowledged, the practical value of this view will then be perceived and confessed.

For all who desire to rid themselves of the society of evil spirits, and to come internally into fellowship with the angels, will see the absolute necessity, not only of a good outward or moral life, but of cleansing "the *inside* of the cup and of the platter"—of acting from right *motives*—of making the love of use, or the desire to serve others from love to the Lord and the neighbor, their ruling principle of action. To this exalted state, therefore, will they aspire. For this they will long; for this they will labor; for this they will pray.

And fully conscious that they cannot attain to this state of right *desire and feeling*, as well as of right *living*, by their own unaided strength, they will be led to look beseechingly to, and humbly to acknowledge their dependence upon Him who hath all power in heaven and on earth; and who has said, "Without me, ye can do nothing."

XIII.

HOW TO ESCAPE HELL.

WE have seen that hell, according to the New Theology, is not a *place* to which a certain class of people are at last sent against their will, as disorderly people in this world are sent to the lock-up, or criminals to the penitentiary; but that it is a *state or quality of life* which each one freely chooses, and which he strengthens or confirms by habit. It is a low condition of humanity—a disorderly or inverted condition—one in which the higher part of our nature is in absolute subjection to the lower, the human to the bestial, the angelic to the infernal. It is not a state of unmitigated misery; for every kind of love, as we have seen, has its delights. The more unselfish is the love that we develop and strengthen—the more it is like God's own love, so much the sweeter and more heavenly is the delight felt in its exercise, and so much the purer and more exalted our happiness; but the more *un*like we are to God in character, feeling and purpose—the more supremely selfish we grow to be, and the more indifferent to the wants and woes and welfare of others, the lower is the form of

life or quality of love developed in the soul, and the
nearer, therefore, does the delight experienced in its exercise, approach to the delights of some of the brute
creation—to the delights of serpents, tigers, dogs and
swine.

In the natural world nothing is positively evil *per se*.
All things are good and useful *in their proper places*.
The ordure from our barns and stables, the filth and
refuse of our filthiest cities, the droppings of wild or
domestic fowls, and even the dead and decomposing
bodies of animals—offensive and hateful as all such things
are when out of place, in our parlors or libraries—are excellent in the field or garden; and in the hands of the
skillful florist or agriculturist, may be turned to profitable
account.

So, too, all the implanted instincts and proclivities of
our natural humanity, including even the love of self
with all its numerous offspring, are not wrong or sinful
per se.   They are all of them gifts of God, and in their
proper place are good and useful.   But what *is* their
proper place?   Not that of rulers, but of servants.
Dogs and horses would make poor masters; but as servants subject to man's direction and control, they are
very useful.   In the order of man's creation, the body
comes first.   Next the bodily senses are developed;
then the lower parts of the mind—those lying nearest
the body—the selfish and sensual propensities; then the
knowing and intellectual faculties; then the rational and

religious. And the highest or God-like part of his nature—the spiritual and truly human—the angel (for this
is "the measure of a man," Rev. xxi. 17) is unfolded last
of all. But this takes place only when the man is " born
from above," or created anew in the image of his Maker.
In this case, none of the passions or propensities of the
natural man are destroyed, but simply brought under subjection to the spiritual and more regal part of his nature
—to the true and heaven-born man. In due subjection
and subordination to the divine human love, everything
belonging to the natural man is good and useful.

This is plainly taught in the spiritual sense of the very
first chapter of the Bible; in which sense this chapter
treats of a spiritual creation, that is, of the normal development of the human soul from its natural, dark, chaotic
state, into one of heavenly order and life—into the image
and likeness of God himself. Note the order in this
creation. First, we have the earth without form, and
void,—and darkness brooding over it. Then comes the
grass, and the herb yielding seed, and the fruit-tree yielding fruit. Then the fishes and the fowls—the "living
creatures which the waters brought forth abundantly after
their kind, and every winged fowl after his kind." Then
"the beast of the earth after his kind, and cattle after
their kind, and everything that creepeth upon the earth
after his kind." And last of all the *man*—a living soul
—created in the image and likeness of his Maker.

"So God created man in his own image; in the

image of God created He him; male and female created
He them.

"And God blessed them; and God said unto them,
Be fruitful, and multiply, and replenish the earth and
subdue it; and have dominion over the fish of the sea,
and over the fowl of the air, and over every living thing
that moveth upon the earth. . . .

"And God saw everything that He had made; and
behold it was very good."

When truth in the understanding becomes firmly
wedded to love in the will, or in other words, when the
great law of unselfish love (which is the properly *human*
life) comes to reign throughout the soul, having complete
dominion over all the feelings, inclinations and thoughts
of the natural mind, then the true *man* is created—the
properly human understanding and will. "Male and
female created He them, and called *their* name Adam,"
that is, *man*. And when this is the case—when all the
instincts, feelings, thoughts and propensities of the natural man are brought under perfect subjection to the
great law of love, then *everything* is seen to be "very
good." The inclinations of the natural man are evil
only when they are allowed to rule. In a state of proper
subordination and subserviency to the celestial principle
—the truly human—they all are very good.

But this exalted and heavenly state, when the soul is
so filled and pervaded by the Divine spirit that it may
truly be said to be created "in the image of God,"

cannot be suddenly attained. Many previous states must be passed through—states of inward labor, and conflict with the foes of "our own household." These states, however, are all indispensable to the final evolution or creation of the *man;* and are what is meant in the spiritual sense by the six days of creation spoken of in Genesis. Accordingly Swedenborg says:

"During regeneration the cupidities and falsities [of the natural man] cannot be instantly removed; for that would be to destroy the whole man, seeing that the life of these is the only life he has yet acquired. Therefore evil spirits are permitted to continue with him for some time, that they may excite his cupidities. . . . And unless the Lord defended man every moment, yea, even the smallest part of a moment, he would instantly perish in consequence of the indescribably intense and mortal hatred which prevails in the world of spirits against the things relating to love and faith toward the Lord.

"The times and states of man's regeneration in general and in particular, are divided into six, and are called the days of his creation. For by degrees he is elevated out of a state in which he possesses none of the qualities which properly constitute a *man,* until by little and little he attains to the sixth day, in which he becomes an image of God.

"During this period the Lord fights continually for him against evils and falsities, and by means of [these internal and spiritual] conflicts confirms him in the true

17 *

and the good. The time of the warfare is the time of
the Lord's operation; therefore a regenerate person is
called by the prophets, *the work of God's fingers*. And
he does not rest until love becomes his ruling principle;
then the conflict ceases. When the work has so far pro-
gressed that faith is united to love, it is then called *very
good;* for the Lord then treats him as a likeness of himself. At the end of the sixth day the evil spirits depart,
and the good ones draw near."—*Arcana Cœlestia*, 59–63.

Then comes the sabbath of the soul;—that state of
inward peace and rest which resembles the sweet and
serene peace of heaven;—a state in which the natural
man yields a perfect and cheerful submission to the
spiritual, or what is the same, to the will of the Heavenly Father. Of this state, Swedenborg speaks thus:

" What the tranquillity of peace of the external man is,
on the cessation of conflict, or when he is no longer dis-
turbed by evil desires and false persuasions, can be known
only to one who is acquainted with the state of peace.
So delightful is this state as to exceed every conception
of delight. Not only is it a cessation of conflict, but life
proceeding from an interior peace, and affecting the external man in a manner that cannot be described."—
Ibid. 92.

What it is, according to the New Theology, to escape
hell, must by this time be obvious. It is to escape, or
rise out of, that low state in which the selfish propensities of the natural man—pride, avarice, ambition, love

of ease or pleasure, lust of power or glory—have complete dominion in the heart, and to come into that exalted and truly human state in which love to the Lord and neighbor have supreme control. And this is something which cannot be suddenly accomplished. It is a life-long work.

And how shall we do it? How is the spiritual to gain the ascendency over the natural man? How, from loving self and the world supremely, shall we be brought into a state to love the Lord above all else, and our neighbor as ourselves? For to undergo this change, is to be lifted out of a hellish into a heavenly state. In other words, it is to escape hell, and enter upon the state denoted by heaven. It is to experience such an inward renewal or change of character, that when we enter the other world we shall loathe and shun the society of devils, and be drawn by the force of spiritual attraction to that of the angels.

How to do this, is the question of questions. Yet the Lord has pointed out the way, and made it very plain to all who are willing to walk in it. He says: "If thou wilt enter into life, keep the commandments." But this, on account of our hereditary selfishness, requires the practice of much self-denial, and the endurance of many inward conflicts with the foes of our own household. The cross is the symbol of these conflicts; and engaging in them, therefore, is what is meant in the spiritual sense by "taking up the cross." Hence the Lord says:

"If any man will come after me, let him deny himself, and take up his cross, and follow me.   For whosoever will save his life, shall lose it; and whosoever will
lose his life for my sake, shall find it."

Our *true* life is the heavenly life—the life of pure unselfish love—the Lord's own life in us, yet perceived as ours.
We *find* or receive this life, only as we overcome or *lose*
our hereditary selfish life for the Lord's sake; and this
we can do only by denying to our natural and inordinate
love of self the gratification which it craves, and engaging in many a fierce conflict with the evil inclinations
which spring from that love.   This is the way the Lord
himself overcame the evil in his assumed humanity, and
made that humanity Divine.   And we, if we would follow Him, or come into full sympathy and spiritual union
with Him (and without this there is no heaven for us),
must do the same.   That is, we must deny self, and take
up our cross.

"Keep the commandments," was the blessed Saviour's
answer to the young man who "came and said unto
Him, Good Master, what good thing shall I do that I
may have eternal life?"   And to every inquirer in every
age, He returns the self-same answer.   And He goes
further and specifies the commandments that are to be
kept: "Thou shalt do no murder: Thou shalt not commit adultery: Thou shalt not steal: Thou shalt not bear
false witness: Honor thy father and thy mother: And
thou shalt love thy neighbor as thyself."

Now the commandments may be kept—in the letter, at least—by one in whom there is no acknowledgment of the Lord, and no sense of dependence on Him. A man may refrain from falsehood, theft, adultery, murder, etc., from purely selfish and worldly considerations;—from fear of the law, or of losing his property or reputation, or from hope of winning the good esteem of others. He may keep all the commandments of the Decalogue, in the outward form, with a heart brim full of pride and self-conceit. He may do it in the spirit of the self-righteous Pharisee, who thanked God that he was so much better than other men. Those who keep the commandments in this spirit, are deficient in one essential qualification for the kingdom of heaven. They lack humility. They lack a sense of utter dependence on the Lord for whatever good they do, or whatever power they have to shun evil. They abound in self-righteousness. All the good they do, they regard as their own, and claim merit on account of it. Some of this class have "great possessions"—large investments in meritorious deeds.

This was the spirit in which that young man had kept the commandments. "All these things," he says, "have I kept from my youth up: What lack I yet?" And what was the Lord's answer? "If thou wilt be perfect, go and sell that thou hast and give to the poor, and thou shalt have treasure in heaven; and come follow me. But when the young man heard that saying, he went away sorrowful; for he had great possessions.''

We may keep the commandments, then, or shun the deeds which they forbid, yet in such a proud spirit or from such selfish motives, that we shall *not* be shunning hell at the same time. We may shun fraud, falsehood, theft, adultery, etc., merely from fear of the law, or of some personal or worldly loss. In that case we shun the evil from prudential considerations, not because it is wrong or sinful in itself; and this is not really shunning the evil at all.

If, therefore, we would shun hell, we must keep the commandments from a religious ground. We must regard the evils which they forbid, as sins against God, and shun them *because they are sins.* If our self-love prompts us to deceive or defraud our neighbor, or to take any undue advantage of his weakness or ignorance, or to injure him in any way, we must regard and shun the doing of such wrong *as a sin.* If we are in the habit of using profane language—of taking the Lord's name in vain—we must regard and shun this habit, not merely because it is ungentlemanly or disreputable, but *because it is sinful.* If we are inclined to deprive another, without his knowledge or consent, of anything that justly belongs to him—be it honor, property, reputation, social position, political or religious influence—we must regard and shun such robbery *as a sin.* If we are inclined to speak evil of others, to slander them—which is a kind of moral murder, for it is stabbing one in the dark—we must inwardly acknowledge the sinfulness of this before God, and shun it *because it is a sin.* If we are inclined to invade the freedom and trample on the rights of others, to domineer over them—over our families, our children, our brethren, our domestics, our employés—to compel them to do *our* will and gratify *our* wishes, to their own injury, loss, or discomfort, we must regard such disposition as sinful, and shun its indulgence *as a sin.*

And so with every inclination which originates in the love of self, and whose indulgence is condemned by the Lord's commandments, being utterly contrary to their whole spirit and teaching. These inclinations are all of them but streams which flow from hell; and their existence and craving are indications of the presence of hell within us. And it is only when we regard and shun their indulgence as *a sin against God,* that we are really shunning hell.

According to the New View, then, as herein unfolded, the way to escape hell becomes very plain. We must first have a clear perception and a firm conviction of what hell really is. We must recognize it as a *state,* and must understand the nature of that state. That is, we must know what kind of life or love belongs to it.

And the next thing necessary is, a sincere desire to be delivered from this state. And since we have no power to deliver ourselves—for no man can of himself change his ruling love—we must rely on One who alone is able to deliver; we must look to Him and pray to Him who hath "all power in heaven and on earth." No one ever was or ever can be delivered from a state of bondage to evil or the love of self, without first *desiring* to be delivered. And a sincere desire for deliverance, implies a perception and acknowledgment of the low state in which we are, and from which we seek to be delivered.

But the desire alone, however intense, is not enough. Prayer for deliverance, however earnest, is not enough. Confession of our clearly discerned selfishness and sin, however penitent, is not enough. Necessary as all these are, they are of no avail without *a life of practical obedience* to the Divine precepts. "Not every one that saith unto me, Lord, Lord," says the great Teacher, "shall enter into the kingdom of heaven; but he that *doeth the will* of my Father which is in heaven." We enter into the kingdom of heaven, just in the degree that we enter into that state of love to the Lord and the neighbor, which is the essential thing in that kingdom. And we enter that state by keeping the commandments, that is, by *doing* the heavenly Father's will; and a part of this consists in shunning, as sins against Him, the things which are contrary to his will.

To come out of darkness, is to come into light. To escape sickness, is to enjoy health. To get rid of weakness, is the same as coming into the possession of strength.

And to escape hell, is to come into the opposite kingdom
—heaven.

"If thou wilt enter into life, keep the commandments." This is the only way—the way pointed out by
God's own finger—to escape hell and reach heaven.
"The commandments" are the laws of the heavenly
life. For all life has its laws; and it is only by con-
formity to these, that the blessings of any kind of life can
be enjoyed.

Take, for example, our corporeal life. This has its
laws; and these laws must be obeyed if we expect to enjoy physical health. Our bodies require food, and
drink, and exercise, and sleep, and pure air, and protection from rain and frost. These requirements are
the body's laws—unchangeable, God-appointed laws.
And in the degree that they are transgressed, the body
suffers. And this suffering is the penalty with which
the Framer of our bodies visits such transgression. The
transgression and the suffering, the violation and the
penalty, are inseparably connected, like cause and
effect.

And the soul, too, has its laws, as well as the body.
And these can no more be violated with impunity, than
can the laws which preside over our physical organism.
In the violation of spiritual as in that of physical laws,
a penalty follows with undeviating certainty;—not a penalty arbitrarily inflicted, or in the way that human tri-
bunals punish offenders against civil enactments, but a

18

penalty linked with transgression as effects are linked with causes.

But that higher life of the soul which those come into who escape hell—the life which we call heavenly—the life which allies us to God and the angels—that which the Scripture calls "eternal life," whose very breath is that unselfish love enjoined by the two great commandments—that life has to be begotten, formed, developed, born in us, generally after the corporeal life has reached maturity. This is the new birth—the birth into a higher, even the heavenly state—to which our Lord has reference when He says: "Except a man be born again, he cannot see the kingdom of God."

How does this new birth of the soul take place? or how is this higher life developed and matured? In the same way that art-life, mechanical ingenuity, industrial skill, oratorical or mathematical power, is developed and perfected. Each follows as the normal result of self-compelled obedience to certain principles or laws.

Ask those who have attained a proud distinction as poets, artists, mechanics, scholars, statesmen, how they won their lofty eminence. And they will tell you that, under God, they are indebted mainly to their own persistent efforts;—to their ceaseless study, their tireless industry, their resolute struggles, their unflinching perseverance, their unremitting toil. They labored while others lounged. They studied while others slept. They were busy while others were idle. They were climbing up the mountain while others were reposing in bowers of ease.

No: Eminence in any art or profession was never achieved in any other way than through the individual's own voluntary and persevering efforts;—through the patient learning and faithful application of the rules of that art or profession.

And so we may say, men are born into the kingdom of heaven—that is, born saints or angels, in the same way that they are born artists, mechanics, scholars, statesmen. For they inherit naturally the capacity or aptitude for each of these; and some have by inheritance a larger capacity or aptitude than others. But they *become* neither the one nor the other without personal effort and much self-imposed labor;—without first learning certain principles or laws, and then reducing these laws to practice.

Take, for illustration, the accomplished musician. How has he become such? He inherited the talent or aptitude for music, just as we all have inherited the capability of becoming angels. He has the musical talent while yet a child—but undeveloped. And so we may say the musician is there *in potency*. But as yet he is in embryo. The individual is all unconscious of his latent powers;—as unconscious of the sweet entrancing delights which the music now wrapped up and hidden within him will one day produce, as an infant before birth is unconscious of its yet latent capabilities, or of the joys of its post-natal state. Properly speaking, the musician is not yet born. He has only an embryonic or latent existence in that individual, like that of the angel in the unregenerate man.

Observe, now, the manner of his birth,—for this will illustrate the manner in which every one who becomes regenerate, is born from above and becomes a true child of God. It will show us how we are to be brought out of the state in which we love ourselves supremely, into the opposite state of love to the Lord and the neighbor; or how "the new man" created in the image of the Lord Jesus Christ, comes forth from "the old man" that is "corrupt according to the deceitful lusts." In a word, it will show us how hell is to be escaped and heaven gained.

First, that individual places himself, or is placed, under the instruction of a Master. He becomes a pupil —a disciple or learner. He takes lessons of a music-teacher. He acquaints himself with the rules of the art —certain musical laws— and then reduces these rules to practice. He does not learn all the rules at once, but only a few, and the very simplest at first. When he has practiced these for a time, then he learns other and more difficult rules; and straightway proceeds to reduce these also to practice.

Thus he goes on, learning and practicing the rules of the art. But he finds little pleasure in these first lessons. He compels himself, however, to go through with them.

It is all labor, task-work, drudgery, in the outset, which he performs reluctantly and without one thrill of delight, yet with the hope of some day becoming a musician. How stiff and clumsy his fingers are at first! How slowly and awkwardly they hobble over the keys, like a child just beginning to walk! How much more readily they go wrong than right! And he finds it vastly more difficult to *practice* the rules, than to commit them to memory. But he struggles on, sometimes hopeful, sometimes discouraged.

At last, by dint of patience and perseverance and much hard parctice, the difficulties are all overcome. The musical laws are incarnated in him. They flow out from the tips of his fingers the moment he seats himself at the instrument. He is now able to render with facility and effect the most difficult compositious of Beethoven or Mozart. And he finds, too, that by practicing, and thereby learning to give faithful expression to, the laws that govern in the realm of music, he becomes more and more enamored with the art. Strange and unlooked for raptures transport him. He is introduced, as it were, into a new world. Sweet melodies are rippling all around him. His soul is flooded with the charms of music. He experiences a delight in executing, or in listening to the execution of, some grand composition, of which, at the beginning of his musical education he could form no conception.

It is in this way that the musician is born; and in

18 *   O

no other. He comes forth, not suddenly nor in any miraculous manner; but slowly, gradually, after years of hard study, close application and unremitting toil. The student learns certain musical rules or laws, and then *compels himself* to reduce those rules to practice. And so at last the musician is produced, developed, formed, or born.

And the painter, sculptor, architect, and mechanic are born in the same way. Each of these comes forth, generally not until the physical man has attained maturity. The individual first makes himself acquainted with the rules of the art, and then learns, through patient and protracted effort, to reduce these rules to practice.

And in a way precisely similar is "the new man" or angel born. In other words, we are introduced or born in a similar manner, into a state of supreme love to the Lord and the neighbor;—are lifted out of that low natural state, which is hell, into that high spiritual state, which is heaven. And this is what is meant by being "born again," "born of the Spirit," "born from above," and "born of God," whereof the Bible speaks.

The only possible way, therefore, of escaping the hellish and attaining unto the heavenly state, is, by first learning the laws of the higher or heavenly life, and then (in humble acknowledgment of our utter and constant dependence on the Lord) reducing them to practice. These laws are all contained in the Sacred Scripture, and are full of the Saviour's own life which is love.   But they must be reduced to practice—they must be religiously obeyed— they must be made the laws of our life, before we may hope to experience the love and delight that are wrapped up within them.

We cannot, of course, learn and practice all these laws at once. That is not expected or required of us. But we are to do it by little and little, just as Raphael learned to paint and Mozart to play. And the task of learning the laws of our higher life, or of receiving truths into the understanding merely, is comparatively easy. Obeying them—living them—practicing them, in the parlor, in the kitchen, in the office, in the shop, in the counting-house, in the market-place, in the school-room, on the farm, at the fire-side, and in legislative halls— everywhere and always conforming our dispositions and conduct to their requirements, and so weaving these laws into the very fabric of our spiritual being, and making them, as it were, a part of ourselves—this is the laborious and difficult part of the work. And so it is with every art, trade or profession. *Learning* the rules is comparatively easy; reducing them to *practice*, is a task of far greater difficulty.

Hence we may see why *doing* the truth is so often urged and so strongly emphasized in the Sacred Scripture. "Blessed are they that *do* his commandments, that they may have right to the tree of life." "Why call ye me Lord, Lord, and *do not* the things which I say?" "My mother and my brethren are those who hear the

Word of God and *do* it." "Whosoever heareth these
sayings of mine and *doeth* them, I will liken unto a wise
man who built his house upon a rock." But "whosoever heareth and *doeth them not*, shall be likened unto
a foolish man who built his house upon the sand." Whosoever *doeth* the will of the Heavenly Father," shall
enter into the Kingdom.

It is impossible, therefore, to escape hell and win
heaven through *faith alone;* that is, by simply learning,
understanding, and believing the truth. Only those who
religiously *do* as the laws of the heavenly life require,
can hope ever to attain unto that life, or to have an inward experience of its joys.

And the first steps in the way of obedience, are, like
all first steps, the most difficult. They have to be taken
from a sense of duty—taken laboriously, with an effort,
through self-compulsion, and without one throb of heavenly delight. They have to be taken when our natural
inclinations urge us in the opposite direction. But as
we go on *practicing* the laws of the higher life, every
successive step becomes easier and more delightful. And
as obedience becomes more and more the habit of the
soul, hell and its delights recede, and the life and joy
of heaven flow in with continually increasing fullness.

No: not by faith alone, or by a mere knowledge and
acknowledgment of the truth, can a man ever escape
hell or reach heaven; but by yielding a voluntary,
though at first a *self-compelled*, obedience to the laws of

heavenly life. Through obedience to these laws—at the same time acknowledging the Lord as their source, and the source of all our disposition and power to obey them —the interiors of the soul are opened toward heaven, and the influx of hell is lessened, and the Lord's life flows in with ever-increasing power and fullness; precisely as, through obedience to the laws of our physical life, physical debility and disorder recede, and bodily health, strength and elasticity flow in.

We cannot love the Lord supremely and our neighbor as ourselves, by simply desiring or willing to do so;— no, nor by the power of faith alone however strong, or prayer however sincere and fervent. But this love is sure to flow into our hearts in the degree that we humbly acknowledge its source, and compel ourselves to obey its laws. Shun falsehood, fraud, deceit, adultery—all known evils—*as sins against God*, and by degrees you will come to hate and loathe these vices. Devote yourself religiously to some useful calling, and you will gradually grow into the love of that use. Practice the laws of charity, and the life of charity with its delights will be imparted unto you more and more. Obey the law of kindness, and there will be a constantly increasing influx of the spirit of kindness into your heart. Do justly, because such is the will of God, and you will grow more and more in love with justice. In all your dealings and intercourse with your fellow men, be careful to obey the laws of neighborly love, and to regard and shun their infraction as a sin, and that love with its unspeakable delights will flood your soul more and more.

But pursue the opposite course—disregard the laws of the soul's higher life—violate the precepts of heavenly charity—trample on the rules of love and justice in your intercourse with your fellows, and your soul will become emptied of the Lord's life, and more and more insensible to its ineffable sweetness; your love of self will grow continually stronger, and your heart more and more like the nether mill-stone; your sympathies will become more contracted and deadened; your sense of justice will grow more and more benumbed; your moral perceptions more and more beclouded; your appreciation of, and your aspirations after, the gifts and graces of heaven, more and more feeble; and the angel life in you become more and more marred and crushed, and the demon life more vigorous and flourishing.

And thus will your soul, created with the capacity of endless progress in wisdom, holiness, and love, and with boundless capabilities of enjoyment, be lost and ruined. Yes—*lost and ruined;* because, through your voluntary neglect or infraction of the revealed and everlasting laws of love—the laws of your soul's higher life, that life is dwarfed and spoiled, or fails to become developed within you. Having *chosen* darkness rather than light, you cannot help missing the glorious boon which you were made capable of attaining—Heaven and its unutterable delights. Verily, saith the Lord:

" What shall it profit a man if he shall gain the whole world and lose his own soul ? Or what shall a man give in exchange for his soul ?"

The nature of heaven and of hell is revealed. The way of escape from one and of entrance into the other, is made plain. The Lord ever watches, and waits, and strives to draw all unto Himself. But He uses no compulsion. He *cannot force* one soul to heaven. He leaves us all in perfect freedom ; and says to every one :

" I have set before you life and death, blessing and cursing. Therefore choose life, that both thou and thy seed may live :

" That thou mayest love the Lord thy God, that thou mayest obey his voice, and that thou mayest cleave unto Him ; for He is thy life, and the length of thy days."

Each one is free to choose for himself. He must and *does* choose for himself.

"And if it seem evil unto you to serve the Lord, choose you this day whom ye will serve."

THE END.

Words in Season. A Manual of Instruction,

Comfort and Devotion for Family Reading and Private Use. By REV. HENRY B. BROWNING, M. A. 16mo. Toned paper. Extra cloth. $1.

"*Words in Season* is the title of a beautiful little volume of practical religious counsels of instruction, comfort and devotion for family reading and private use. It appears to be truly evangelical, and to be calculated, in style and spirit, to do the good at which it aims."—*Boston Congregationalist.*

"*Words in Season,* a thoughtful, sweet-toned manual for family reading and hours of devotion, prepared by an English minister of the Established Church Spiritual souls will read it with comfort and strengthening."—*Chicago Advance.*
"A very good book."—*N. Y. Liberal Christian.*

The Scriptural Doctrine of Hades. Comprising

an Inquiry into the State of the Righteous and Wicked Dead between Death and the General Judgment, and demonstrating from the Bible that the Atonement was neither made on the Cross nor yet in this World. By REV. GEORGE BARTLE, D. D., Principal of Walton College, Liverpool. 12mo. Cloth. $1.50.

"Appears to be to demonstrate that Christ actually descended into hell after death; that the time intervening between his death and his resurrection was spent there not in preaching to the lost spirits, but in actually suffering their punishment; and that this actual and literal suffering of the 'second death' was necessary to complete the atonement and to make him a true and sufficient substitute for

sinners. We shall not attempt to follow the elaborate argument by which the author endeavors to sustain this most extraordinary position. . . . . Giving to the author credit for very considerable research and no little ingenuity in the construction of his argument, we must, nevertheless, rank his book as among the 'curiosities of literature.'"—*N. Y. Independent.*

Our Children in Heaven. By William H. Hol-

COMBE, M. D., author of "The Sexes," etc. 12mo. Tinted paper. Extra cloth. $1.75.

"Its sweet pathos and comforting sympathy at once warm and interest us."—*Albany Journal.*

"It is written in the most devout spirit, and will interest even those who reject its doctrines."—*Buffalo Express.*

The Sexes: Here and Hereafter. By William

H. HOLCOMBE, M. D., author of "Our Children in Heaven," etc. 12mo. Tinted paper. Extra cloth. $1.50.

"Whatever one may think of the doctrines of this book, it would be impossible to deny that it breathes a pure and elevated spirit, and has many thoughts

which will commend themselves sympathetically to the followers of all Christian faiths."—*The Independent, N. Y.*

In Both Worlds. By Wm. H. Holcombe, M. D.,

author of "Our Children in Heaven," "The Sexes: Here and Hereafter," etc., etc. 12mo. Tinted paper. Extra cloth. $1.75.

"While likely to prove of the deepest and most thrilling interest to all whose minds are elevated above materiality and

the grosser elements of nature, it is in no sense irreverent."—*Boston Evening Traveler.*

Mistaken; or, The Seeming and the Real. 'By LYDIA FULLER. 12mo. Fine cloth, $1.50.

*Moody Mike; or, The Power of Love. A Christ*mas Story. By FRANK SEWALL. Illustrated. 16mo. Extra cloth, $1.

Talks with a Philosopher on the Ways of God to Man. By the author of "Talks with a Child on the Beatitudes." 16mo. Cloth.

Lessons from Daily Life. By Emily E. Hildreth. 12mo. Tinted paper. Extra cloth, $1.

The Other Life. By Dr. W. H. Holcombe, author of "The Sexes," "In Both Worlds," etc. 12mo. Cloth.

Who was Swedenborg? By O. P. Hiller. 16mo. Paper cover, 25 cents. Cloth, 50 cents.

Letters to a Man of the World. By J. F. E. LE BOYS DES GUAYS, ex-sous Prefect in Department du cher. Revised edition. 16mo. Cloth, $1.50.

Doctrine of Life for the New Jerusalem; from the Commandments of the Decalogue. By EMANUEL SWEDEN-BORG. 24mo. Extra cloth, gilt, 75 cents.

Heroism. By Horace Field. 12mo. *Extra cloth,* $1.50.

Thoughts in my Garden. By Mary G. Ware, author of "Elements of Character," etc. 16mo. Cloth, $1.25.

Death and Life. By Mary G. Ware, author of "Thoughts in my Garden," etc. 16mo. Cloth, $1.25.

Lectures on the New Dispensation signified by the New Jerusalem; designed to unfold and elucidate the leading doctrines of the New Church. By Rev. B. F. BARRETT. 12mo. Cloth, $1.50.

Letters on the Divine Trinity, addressed to Henry Ward Beecher. By Rev. B. F. BARRETT. New and enlarged edition. 12mo. Extra cloth, $1.25.

The Divine Attributes. Including also the Divine Trinity. A Treatise on the Divine Love and Divine Wisdom, and Correspondence. From the "Apocalypse Explained" of Emanuel Swedenborg. 12mo. Extra cloth, $2.

Angelic Wisdom Concerning the Divine Love and Wisdom. By EMANUEL SWEDENBORG. From the original Latin as edited by Dr. J. F. I. Tafel. Translated by R. N. Foster. Demi 8vo. Extra cloth, $2.

Heaven and its Wonders, and Hell. From Things Heard and Seen. By EMANUEL SWEDENBORG. From the Latin edition of Dr. J. F. I. Tafel. Translated by B. F. Barrett. Demi 8vo. Extra cloth, $2.50.

Angelic Wisdom Concerning the Divine Provi- dence. By EMANUEL SWEDENBORG. From the original Latin as edited by Dr. J. F. I. Tafel. Translated by R. Norman Foster. Demi 8vo. Tinted paper. Extra cloth, $2.25.

True Christian Religion. Containing the entire Theology of the New Church, foretold by the Lord in Dan vii. 13 14 and Rev. xxi. 1, 2. By EMANUEL SWEDENBORG. From the Latin edition of Dr. J. F. I. Tafel. Translated by R. Norman Foster. 2 vols. demi 8vo. Tinted paper. Extra cloth, $5.

Life and Works of Emanuel Swedenborg. By W. WHITE. With Four Steel Plates. 8vo. Extra cloth, $5.

Life of Emanuel Swedenborg, with a Synopsis of his Writings. By W. WHITE. With an Introduction by Rev. B. F. Barrett. 12mo. Extra cloth, $1.50.

Life : Its Nature, Varieties and Phenomena. By LEO H. GRINDON, author of "Emblems," "Figurative Language," etc. First American Edition. 12mo. Extra cloth, $2.25.

Talks with a Child on the Beatitudes. By the

author of "Talks with a Philosopher." 16mo. Fine cloth, 75 cents. Cloth, flexible, 50 cents.

"A volume written in a sweet, devout, simple and tender spirit, and calculated to edify the old as well as the young."—*Boston Ev. Transcript.*

"A charming little volume to place in the hands of young people."—*Boston Journal.*

Deus Homo : God-Man. By Theophilus Parsons.

Crown 8vo. Extra cloth, $2.50.

"Perhaps no book has appeared from the scholars of the New Church that has promised more light to the inquirer or be-

stowed more satisfaction upon the reader."—*Historical Magazine.*

Emanuel Swedenborg as a Philosopher and a Man

of Science. By R. L. TAFEL. Crown 8vo. Extra cloth, $2.25.

"We invite our readers to peruse Prof. Tafel's book. Its reading will acquaint them with one of the greatest thinkers and

one of the purest characters that ever lived."—*St. Louis Paper.*

Elements of Character. By Mary G. Ware,

author of "Death and Life," etc. 16mo. Cloth, $1.25.

"This work is entitled to a place among

the higher productions of American female literature."—*Harper's Magazine.*

Observations on the Growth of the Mind. By

SAMPSON REED. Seventh edition. 16mo. Extra cloth, $1.

"The title of the work expresses its character. It is an attempt to show *how the mind grows,* and after defining the essential character of the mind the author

points out, in a most interesting and original manner, the actual development required."—*Boston Transcript.*

Observations on the Authenticity of the Gospels.

By a Layman. Second edition. 16mo. Extra cloth, $1.

"A work that should be in everybody's library, and especially ought steps to be immediately taken to place it in the hands

of every theological student in our land."—*Religious Magazine.*
"The author writes with vigor and clearness."—*North American Review.*

Sermons on the Lord's Prayer. By Henry A.

WORCESTER. 12mo. Cloth, $1.25.

www.ingramcontent.com/pod-product-compliance
Lightning Source LLC
Chambersburg PA
CBHW030134030726
47498CB00007B/2707